"I need a fiancée."

Rafik gave Anne a rueful smile. "I don't mean a real fiancée. Though that's what my father wants for me. He thinks I should get married and settle down. I'm against that plan. What I'm looking for is someone who's willing to pose as my fiancée for a short time."

"So what's the problem?" Anne replied. "How could a woman say no to a charming man like you?"

"Perhaps you'd consider…"

"Me?" Her eyes widened. "You thought I would pose as your fiancée? Why would I do that?"

"I thought after reflecting on that night we spent together, the hours we shared…you might feel differently about me."

She stared at him. "According to you, nothing happened that night we spent together. That's what you said. Nothing happened. Now I want to know the truth."

"Ah, the truth. All I can say is that it was the most incredible night of my life…."

Dear Reader,

Although it will be archived by now, I've been writing to readers on our www.eHarlequin.com community bulletin boards about Silhouette Romance and what makes it so special. Readers like the emotion, the strength of the heroines, the truly heroic nature of the men and a quick, yet satisfying, read. I'm delighted that Silhouette Romance is able to fulfill a few of your fantasies! Be sure to stop by our site. :)

I hope you had a chance to revisit *Lion on the Prowl* by Kasey Michaels when it was out last month in a special collection with Heather Graham's *Lucia in Love*. Be sure not to miss a glimpse into those characters' lives with this month's lively spin-off called *Bachelor on the Prowl*. Elizabeth Harbison gives us *A Pregnant Proposal* from our continuity HAVING THE BOSS'S BABY. Look out next month for *The Makeover Takeover* by Sandra Paul.

Other stories this month include the second title in Lilian Darcy's THE CINDERELLA CONSPIRACY. Be assured that *Saving Cinderella* has the heartwarming emotion and strong heroes that Lilian Darcy delivers every time! And Carol Grace has spun off a title from *Fit for a Sheik*. This month, look for *Taming the Sheik*.

And we've got a Christmas treat to get you in the mood for the holidays. Carolyn Greene has *Her Mistletoe Man* while new-to-the-line author Holly Jacobs asks *Do You Hear What I Hear?*

I hope that you enjoy these stories, and keep in touch.

Mary-Theresa Hussey

Mary-Theresa Hussey,
Senior Editor

Please address questions and book requests to:
Silhouette Reader Service
U.S.: 3010 Walden Ave., P.O. Box 1325, Buffalo, NY 14269
Canadian: P.O. Box 609, Fort Erie, Ont. L2A 5X3

Taming the Sheik

CAROL GRACE

SILHOUETTE *Romance*®

Published by Silhouette Books

America's Publisher of Contemporary Romance

SILHOUETTE BOOKS

ISBN 0-373-19554-0

TAMING THE SHEIK

Visit Silhouette at www.eHarlequin.com

Printed in U.S.A.

Books by Carol Grace

Silhouette Romance

Make Room for Nanny #690
A Taste of Heaven #751
Home Is Where the Heart Is #882
Mail-Order Male #955
The Lady Wore Spurs #1010
*Lonely Millionaire #1057
*Almost a Husband #1105
*Almost Married #1142
The Rancher and the Lost Bride #1153
†Granted: Big Sky Groom #1277
†Granted: Wild West Bride #1303
†Granted: A Family for Baby #1345
Married to the Sheik #1391
The Librarian's Secret Wish #1473
Fit for a Sheik #1500
Taming the Sheik #1554

Silhouette Desire

Wife for a Night #1118
The Heiress Inherits a
   Cowboy #1145
Expecting... #1205
The Magnificent M.D. #1284

*Miramar Inn
†Best-Kept Wishes

CAROL GRACE

has always been interested in travel and living abroad. She spent her junior year of college in France and toured the world working on the hospital ship *HOPE*. She and her husband spent the first year and a half of their marriage in Iran, where they both taught English. She has studied Arabic and Persian languages. Then, with their toddler daughter, they lived in Algeria for two years.

Carol says that writing is another way of making her life exciting. Her office is her mountaintop home, which overlooks the Pacific Ocean and which she shares with her inventor husband, their daughter, who just graduated college, and their teenage son.

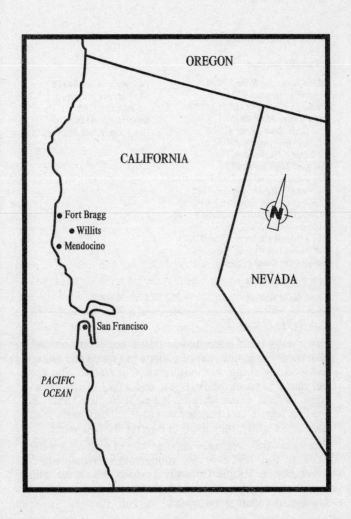

Chapter One

It was the most beautiful wedding of the year. The sun shone through the stained-glass windows of the church atop Nob Hill in San Francisco. The scent of roses filled the air. Bridal consultant Carolyn Evans walked down the aisle to marry Sheik Tarik Oman to the strains of the wedding march played on the magnificent pipe organ. It was an occasion no one would ever forget. Especially bridesmaid Anne Sheridan.

As the groom lifted the bride's veil and kissed her, there wasn't a dry eye in the front row where the family sat. Anne's eyes filled with tears, too. So many they threatened to spill down her cheeks. But it was not because she was overcome with emotion or because her pink silk shoes pinched her toes. It was an allergic reaction. While many people were allergic to grasses and trees, she knew from being tested last year she was allergic to flowers. She was allergic to the peonies and lilies in her bouquet, to the stephanotis at the end of each aisle, and even to the arrangements of roses at the altar.

To prepare for the wedding and guard against sneezing in the middle of the ceremony, she'd asked her doctor for extra-strength antihistamines which she'd taken an hour ago. Even so, her throat was raw and her eyes watered. It was clear she'd need another pill before the flower-filled garden reception to be held at the groom's mansion. Unable to reach for a tissue, she blinked back the tears and bit her lip. She was grateful all eyes were on the bride so no one would notice her red-rimmed eyes and obvious discomfort.

But someone did notice. One of the groomsmen at the altar was staring at her and not the bride. It was one of Sheik Tarik's twin cousins she'd met the night before at the rehearsal dinner. He was good-looking in an exotic way, but she couldn't tell the difference between the twin brothers. They'd both flirted with every woman there except for her. She wasn't the type men flirted with. She was a sane and sensible private-school teacher who stayed in the background and watched the festivities.

Whichever twin he was, he wasn't flirting now, he was just looking at her intently as if he couldn't believe she was getting carried away and crying at her best friend's wedding. He raised one eyebrow, and she knew he must think she was an emotional basket case. As if she cared. After today she'd never see him again. He and his brother were just two of the out-of-town guests here for the wedding and would be leaving soon afterward.

She tore her gaze from his admittedly handsome face and focused on her friend Carolyn, thinking how happy she was for her. Marrying a rich and gorgeous sheik. After years of planning weddings for others, Carolyn was finally able to plan one for herself. And what a wedding it was. Somehow Anne got through the rest of the ceremony without coughing or sneezing and made it down the aisle and out in front of the church where she took a deep breath of fresh air.

"Are you all right?" A deep voice, a hand on her bare shoulder made a shiver go up her spine. Somehow she knew before she turned around. It was him.

"Of course, I'm fine," she said breathlessly, trying to ignore the warmth of his hand on her bare skin. Telling herself the goosebumps that had popped out on her arms were due to the cool air and not his warm touch.

"Look, it's just a wedding. Nothing to cry about," he said. "If anyone's crying it should be Tarik. Losing his freedom. Yes, it's enough to make every man in the place weep." He gave her a good-natured grin and removed his hand from her shoulder.

Immediately she missed the warmth of his touch. Ridiculous. A strange man took his hand away and she felt a chill. She tried to shrug off his remarks, which were obviously those of a confirmed cynic. He was just a typical, macho male with a commitment phobia. "You don't understand," she said. "I wasn't crying...."

"Not crying?" There was amused surprise in his tone. Surprised that she'd try to deny it. Surprised that she'd dared disagree with him. He leaned forward until his face was only inches from hers and studied her carefully. His eyes held her gaze for a long moment. She tried to look away but couldn't. She was trapped in the depths of those deep-brown eyes. Could that be sympathy she saw there or curiosity or something else? All she knew was she felt he was looking deep into her soul and she didn't want him to. After all, she didn't even know him.

He brushed a thumb against her cheekbone to wipe away a tear. A surprisingly gentle touch from a sophisticated man who looked like he came straight out of *GQ*. She felt a quiver run up her spine. Her legs felt like jelly. What was wrong with her, anyway? It must be the wedding, the tears, the joy and the music that were having an effect on her.

Not to mention those allergy pills. No man had ever made her feel like this. No man had ever brushed away her tears either.

"Those were tears there," he continued, cocking his head to one side. "You're not a very good liar, sweetheart. I know what I saw."

Anne took a deep breath and looked around. She had to get away from this man. Just in case it wasn't the music, the tears and the flowers, just in case her condition had something to do with this man, with the way he looked at her, the way his thumb left an imprint on her cheek and the way his hand felt on her shoulder. She had to escape, right now. Before this cousin of the groom jumped to the conclusion that his unwanted attention was affecting her one way or another. That it was because of him she felt cold on the outside and hot on the inside. Or that she was afraid to look into his eyes again, which she absolutely was not.

She didn't know where to go. Looking around, it seemed everyone was with someone. The photographer was snapping candid pictures, people were throwing rice and laughing and talking. No one was looking at her except him. She wished he wouldn't. She wished he'd go join one of those other groups. But he didn't. He just stood there looking at her. As if she were some rare bird like the ones she tracked on their migratory routes.

Thank heavens no one heard him call her "sweetheart" or noticed him touching her. Thank heavens no one knew what an effect that touch had on her. She felt it even now, the brush of his thumb on her skin. What an innocent she was. Any other woman would have shrugged it off, because it didn't mean anything after all. Not to him.

"All right," she said, "you saw tears, but not because...not for the reason you thought."

"Cheer up," he said with a smile that showed a flash of white teeth against his bronzed skin. "Think of it this way, you're not losing a friend, you're gaining a sheik."

"Is that a good thing?" she asked, trying to strike a light-hearted, bantering tone, as if she dealt with handsome sheiks every day of the week. If she did she'd know how to deal with this man who undoubtedly needed a dose of humility. Not that she was the one to teach him. She taught six-year-olds to count and spell and read. She'd never met a sheik until Carolyn introduced her to Tarik, her fiancé, a kind and charming man who was obviously totally different from his cousin.

"A *very* good thing," he said, his dark eyes dancing with fun.

Flirting. That's what he was doing, she realized with a start. He was flirting with her, but she didn't know how to flirt back. So she just stood there staring at him, wondering why he bothered with her. Why not hit on one of the other bridesmaids who'd know what to do, know what to say to a good-looking bachelor on the prowl. Anyone else would know how to put him in his place with a lighthearted riposte.

She was saved from responding to this bit of braggadocio by a request from the photographer for a picture of the entire wedding party inside the church.

"I guess that means me," she said, grateful for the distraction.

"It means *us*," he said, offering his arm.

She smiled weakly. As much as she wanted to, she knew it would be rude to ignore him, to stalk on ahead as if he hadn't spoken, as if he hadn't held out his arm. So she gingerly took his arm, so gingerly that he paused.

"I won't bite, you know," he said, slanting a teasing glance in her direction. Again his eyes danced with fun. At her expense. She didn't know what to say, so she didn't say anything. And they walked back up the aisle of the church. Thank heavens she wasn't a bride, because she stumbled on the red carpet halfway to the altar, which caused the sheik to tighten his grip on her arm. He finally had to let her go so she could take her place with the brides-maids and so he could take his place next to the groom.

But before the flashbulbs starting popping, she was compelled to cast a glance in his direction and found him looking at her. When he caught her eye he winked flirtatiously at her, and she quickly looked away.

Luckily she had to help the bride with her train on the way back down the aisle, and she lost sight of the sheik. Otherwise who knew what would have happened? She might have ridden with him back to the reception. She might have been wedged into one of the limos next to him all the way through town. The thought of his thigh pressed against hers, his shoulder next to hers caused the heat to rise to her head. She paused to take another allergy pill while she gave herself a stern warning about handsome men on the prowl.

Instead of riding with the sheik, luckily she caught a ride to the reception with Carolyn's mother and aunt, during which they oohed and ahhed about what a lovely wedding it was and how beautiful Carolyn looked. Anne agreed enthusiastically, but when they started talking about the twin brothers, Rafik and Rahman, she closed her eyes and leaned back against the leather seat. She didn't want to hear about them and she didn't want to talk about them. She had nothing to say. She didn't even know which one was which. This second dose of allergy medicine made her feel increasingly tired and groggy. If she could just make an appearance at the reception, she'd sneak out early and take a taxi home.

But she couldn't ignore the conversation floating around her in the car. She couldn't help feeling as if she were listening to a dialog from a movie.

"Aren't those twins the handsomest men you've ever seen? You know, they arrived for the wedding a few weeks ago, but I heard they like it so much in San Francisco, they're opening a branch of the family business here," Carolyn's mother said. "They're going to be quite an addition to the social scene. With their looks and their money and their status."

"So handsome," Carolyn's aunt murmured.

"Absolutely adorable, if I were thirty years younger...."

The two women burst into girlish laughter and even Anne had to smile. What was it about weddings that brought out the frivolous in everyone? Everyone but her.

"Anne, dear, how are you?" Carolyn's mother asked anxiously observing her daughter's best friend. "Weddings can be so exhausting. I know I'm going to spend the next week recovering. But you'll feel better once we get to the reception. They've booked the most wonderful band and the caterer is the best in town."

Anne nodded. She was sure everything about the reception would be perfection, if she knew Carolyn. They'd been friends since high school, spending hours together daydreaming about the future. Carolyn sketching bridal gowns, clipping articles on weddings from the society pages, destined for bridal bliss herself. Anne studying hard, determined to be a teacher, picturing herself surrounded by children as she read the stories to them that she'd loved as a child.

When Anne was diagnosed with scoliosis in her sophomore year Carolyn stood by her. She took notes for her friend when she had to miss school for doctor's appointments. Cheered her up when she had to wear a back brace

right up to graduation. Tried to lure her out to parties and
dances. But Anne was shy and unsure of herself around
boys. Who in their right mind would be interested in a girl
in a brace? No one, that's who.

Anne was never jealous of Carolyn. Even now with a
lifetime of happiness ahead of her, Anne only wished her
the best. Carolyn deserved it. After spending years planning
weddings for other people, she'd finally planned her own
to a man she was madly in love with.

Anne was determined to try to enjoy the reception for as
long as she could. The good news was she'd been able to
avoid the groom's cousin completely so far. The bad news
was she was so terribly tired. All she wanted to do right
now was to lie down and take a nap. It was a side effect
of the medicine, she knew. At least her tears had dried up
and she wouldn't be accused of getting emotional over a
wedding.

The house on the bluff above the ocean was beautiful.
The view from the garden was spectacular. Guests were
handed a glass of champagne or sparkling fruit juice as they
arrived at the entrance to the patio. Anne sipped her champagne gratefully. Her mouth was as dry as cotton. She
found a chair half hidden behind a native fern and drained
her glass. She heard voices, saw shapes and forms but
hoped that no one, especially no one from the wedding
party, could see her or they'd ask her what was wrong,
insist she join the party, meet someone and say something.
Never a social butterfly, she had never felt less social than
today.

Suddenly the murmur of voices got louder. Voices she
recognized.

"Say, Carolyn," a familiar male voice said, "have I told
you how beautiful you look? Too bad Tarik saw you first.
He has all the luck."

"I'm the one who's lucky, Rafik. And so happy. One of these days we'll be dancing at your wedding."

"Have you been talking to my father? That's his idea of happiness, not mine. Why get married when there are so many wonderful willing women around. By the way, who's your bridesmaid?"

"Which one?"

"In the pink dress."

"They're all in pink dresses."

"Reddish hair, blue eyes."

"You mean Anne. My best friend from high school. Stay away from her, Rafik. She's a wonderful woman, but she's not willing. And she's too good for a player like you," Carolyn said in a teasing voice.

"Why don't we let her decide?" he asked. "Besides, everything's about to change. I'm going to be in charge of the new office here in San Francisco. I'm afraid my party days are over and my playboy ways are going to be sharply curtailed. Not that I'll ever settle down, but I can't stay out all night partying anymore if I'm going to be in the office at nine every morning. Woe is me."

"You're too much, Rafik. Let me introduce you to Lila. She's a lot of fun."

"I met her. She's fine but not my type. Have you seen Anne around?"

"Rafik, I warned you…" Carolyn sighed. "No, I haven't seen her since the church."

Just as Anne was congratulating herself on her apparent invisibility, the pollen from the flowers that bordered the ferns she was hiding behind overcame her antihistamines and she sneezed.

Carolyn peeked around the plants. "There you are," she said. She and Rafik circled around the ferns and stood looking down at her. "Come on and join the party. You've met Tarik's cousin Rafik, haven't you?"

"Yes, of course, I mean, that is I...I...." she stammered. "Not formally."

Rafik held out his hand and he pulled her to her feet. If it weren't for him she might have fallen over. Her knees wobbled and she felt dizzy. She hoped they wouldn't notice. Carolyn didn't, but then her head was in the clouds. Rafik gave Anne a searching second glance.

"Happy to meet you, Anne," he said, trapping her hand between both of his. She tugged, but he had no intention of letting her go. Maybe it was just as well. Without his support she might have toppled over.

"If you two will excuse me," Carolyn said. "I must say hello to some people. Rafik, remember what I said," she added pointedly.

Anne wanted to go with her. Surely there were people she had to say hello to, too. But she couldn't move. So she stood there, her hand still being held tightly by the sheik who showed no sign of remembering anything Carolyn had said. Why? she asked herself. Why didn't he go off and dance with Lila, why stay with her?

"You look like you could use something to drink," he said, studying her with narrowed eyes.

She nodded. "I'm really thirsty."

"Let's get some champagne and a few of those delicious hors d'oeuvres." He tucked her hand securely under his arm for the second time that day and they strolled over to a table laden with all kinds of delectable canapés. With his support, she felt stronger, more in control.

"Champagne?" she asked. "I didn't know you were permitted to drink."

"My brother and I were sent to boarding school in the U.S. as kids. Then we stayed in this country for university on the east coast since the family business is multinational. I'm afraid we're pretty much Americanized by now. For better or worse.'' Again that disarming grin. The one that charmed all those willing women who were no doubt in his life. ''You notice Tarik is serving fruit juice, too, for those like my parents who observe the religious rules of our country.''

Anne felt much better after she'd eaten two stuffed mushrooms and drunk another glass of champagne. ''I'm fine now,'' she said to the sheik. ''Thank you.'' *You can go now. Don't feel obliged to take care of me.*

''Sure you're all right? Not going to cry anymore?''

''For the last time, I wasn't crying.'' *Goodbye.*

''Right. You notice I didn't mention it to your friend Carolyn.''

''I appreciate that,'' Anne said. ''If you'll excuse me I'm going to uh…I see some friends over there. Nice meeting you.'' If that wasn't a decided exit, she didn't know what was, she thought as she walked slowly across the lawn, her high heels scraping the ground. She didn't turn to see if she'd hurt his feelings. She was sure she wasn't capable of any such thing. He was most likely on his way to find another woman, chat up another bridesmaid, hoping she'd be more receptive to his so-called charm.

Rafik stood watching the woman wobble across the lawn, Carolyn's words ringing in his ears. *A wonderful woman. Stay away from her. Too good for you.*

She was right. Anne was just the type he was not interested in. Shy. Quiet. Emotional. Heaven save him from the weepy kind of women who cry at weddings. Oh, it was okay if you were the mother of the bride or groom. So what was wrong with him, hitting on a woman who was most definitely not his type? There was something about her, the way she tried to hold back the tears that brought out the protector in him. She made him feel admirable. The way she looked at him through damp lashes, cheeks flushed, her face framed in that gorgeous red-gold hair.

He reminded himself he was not interested in being admirable. He was not looking to protect someone. He was looking for a smooth, sexy, smart and sassy woman who could protect herself. Anne Sheridan was none of the above. Besides she was a friend of Carolyn's, his new cousin-in-law whom he respected. Half-reluctantly, he turned and looked over the bevy of lovely women, enough women gathered here to please a whole family of sheiks. For some reason he couldn't seem to focus on any one of them.

"Hey," his brother threw an arm around his shoulders. "Having fun? Who was the lady in pink I saw you with?"

"Just one of the bridesmaids."

"I *know* it was one of the bridesmaids," Rahman said. "What's her name?"

"Anne Sheridan. A friend of Carolyn's. Why?"

"I don't know. Don't remember her from the rehearsal dinner. Thought I'd met every pretty woman there. I might introduce myself. Unless you…?"

"No, absolutely not," Rafik said. "Wouldn't touch her with a ten-foot pole. Not my type. Not yours either."

"Okay. Just asking. What a party, huh?"

It *was* quite a party, and Rafik would have been a fool to miss a moment of it. He threw himself into enjoying the music, the dancing, and oh, yes, chatting up the women. So much so, he almost forgot about the auburn-haired bridesmaid in the pink dress. Out of sight, out of mind. That's the way it always was with him. But in one small corner of his mind during the fun, he wondered what had happened to her. He hoped his brother had followed his advice and ignored her. Not that he really cared. Not that she was his responsibility. It was just that she seemed so fragile and so vulnerable. It was obvious somebody ought to be responsible for her. Just so it wasn't him or anyone he knew.

Yes, he'd all but forgotten about her, until at the end of the afternoon, as dusk was falling over the manicured grounds, after the eating, drinking and dancing, he was called upon to make a toast. He stood on the dance platform in front of the musicians who were packing up and told some anecdotes about Tarik that made everyone laugh. Just as he lifted his glass of champagne to toast his cousin and his bride, he saw Anne at the edge of the crowd. She lifted her glass and caught his eye. She definitely looked like she'd had a few too many glasses of champagne. Funny. He wouldn't have picked her for a lush.

Maybe he ought to bring her a piece of wedding cake and see how she was doing. But when he went looking for her, cake in hand, she was gone. It was just as well.

"Rafik." Carolyn got up from the small table where she was sitting with a group of older people and caught his arm. "Do me a favor, will you? Anne isn't feeling well. Could you give her a ride home?"

"Sure. Where is she?"

"At the front door. She wanted to call a taxi, but I'm a little worried. I want to be sure she gets home all right."

"Okay," he said.

He pulled his car up in front of the house and left the motor running while he bounded up the front steps. He found her standing in the doorway of the house, looking confused.

"Oh," Anne said, startled to see Rafik at the door.

"Come on," he said, putting his arm around her waist.

"I'm waiting for a taxi. Thanks anyway," she said, trying unsuccessfully to disengage his arm.

"I'm the taxi," he said. "I'm taking you home. Orders from Carolyn."

"That's not necessary," she said. Of all people. She did not want to be indebted to this man, who thought he was God's gift to womankind. Who'd already seen her at her worst. She'd managed to avoid him for the past few hours, and now here he was again.

"Really. I'm fine. I just need…." She just needed to lie down and close her eyes. Her head was pounding, the room was spinning, and Rafik's face was going in and out of focus. When he picked her up as easily as if she weighed no more than a rag doll and carried her down the steps to his waiting car, her head bobbed against his shoulder. She pounded him on his back in an attempt to make him let her go, but it had no effect on him at all.

He very carefully installed her in the passenger seat, taking her small clutch bag from her hand and removing her shoes before he tucked her feet in. She sighed. Despite her protests, she had to admit it felt so good to be taken care of. So good to have those tight shoes off. Again she was surprised that a big, broad-shouldered, dashing man-about-town would have such a gentle touch. As he fastened her seat belt, his hand grazed the bodice of her silk dress and she gasped. Her eyes flew open and met his amused gaze.

"Just following the seat-belt law," he said innocently. "Wouldn't want to be stopped for any kind of violation."

"Right," she said.

Did he know, could he tell she was unaccustomed to being touched there? Unused to being touched at all by a man? That just a brush of his hand had left her shaky and breathless? Or was that, too, the effect of the champagne and the medicine? What did it matter? He'd been instructed to take her home and he was doing it. She ought to be grateful.

"Where do you live?" he asked.

"In the Sunset," she said. "Out by the....you know...."
She hoped he knew because the names of the streets of San
Francisco were going round and round in her brain. Such
nice names. Which one was hers? "Octavia. Laguna.
Chestnut. Larkin. Pine and Bush," she murmured.

"What?" he said. "I'm new in town. You'll have to give
me better directions than that."

"Take Geary," she said. "No, no better take California."

"I know California Street," he said confidently. "No
problem. You just relax till we get there."

Relax? She was so relaxed she might never move again.
"Nice car," she said, though all she knew was that it
smelled like leather and the seat was so comfortable she
wanted to stay there forever.

"It's new," he said. "I didn't need a car when we lived
in New York, but I do here," he said. "My life is about
to change. Drastically."

"No more playboy, hmm?"

"Where'd you hear that?" he asked sharply.

"Heard you talking."

"I thought maybe you'd been talking to my father."

She shook her head. Just to utter another word would
require too much effort.

"He thinks it's time I grew up. Took over the business
and got married. I'm the elder son, you know."

"I thought...twins," she murmured.

"Yes, we're twins, but I was born first. By thirty
minutes. So Rahman's allowed some slack while I'm the
heir apparent. I'm the one who gets the corner office. I'm
the one who gets the responsibility of running it. I'm the
one who's supposed to find a wife and settle down. Don't

tell anyone I said that. I'm trying to talk him out of that one.''

As if she could tell anyone anything. Her lips were numb, her eyes refused to open. He was still talking. She could hear the words but they made no sense. None at all.

When Rafik got to California Street he turned to ask Anne which way to turn, but her eyes were closed and she was breathing softly and steadily. She'd fallen asleep.

''Hey, wake up,'' he said. ''Which way on California?'' He shook her gently by the shoulder. Nothing. ''Anne. Where do you live? Come on, sweetheart, speak to me.'' But she didn't. She slid down even farther in the seat. Too much to drink, obviously. Well, it wasn't the first time he'd been stuck with an inebriated date. Though he usually knew where they lived. He could go back to the wedding or call Carolyn, but the truth was, he was tired himself. It had been a week of nonstop pre-wedding parties along with setting up a new office and frankly he was beat. He, the man who loved a good time, who'd never met a party he didn't like, was slowing down. What was the matter with him?

Another thing. He didn't relish telling Carolyn her friend had passed out before he even got her home. It might put a damper on the remainder of the party for her. And it would make her best friend look bad. The only thing to do was take her back to his hotel with him. It was a comfortable suite with great room service and a giant king-sized bed. When she came to, he'd sober her up with coffee, find out where she lived and drive her home.

Unfortunately Anne was still out of it when they arrived at the hotel. How was he going to get her up to his room without causing a scene? He pulled up to the front entrance and tried once more to wake her up. ''We're here,'' he said loudly. ''Come on. Do me a favor and wake up.'' She didn't stir.

The doorman opened the passenger door and waited.

Rafik jumped out of the car and lifted Anne up in his arms.

"Fell asleep in the car," Rafik explained to the blue-uniformed doorman. "She'll be fine. Have the valet park it, will you?"

"Certainly, sir," he said, as if comatose guests arrived every day and had to be carried into the hotel.

The lobby was crowded with well-dressed guests. There was a party going on in one of the ballrooms. Not all of the people turned to stare at the man in the tuxedo carrying a redheaded woman in a strapless pink silk dress to the elevator. But most of them did. The decibel level fell about twenty points as a kind of hush fell over the crowd. The hush was replaced with murmurs.

"*Who* is *that?*"

"One of those sheiks. He shut down the bar the other night. Isn't he too much?"

"No, I mean her. Who's she? I've never seen her before."

"It couldn't be…no, if I didn't know better I'd think it was Emma's teacher, Miss Sheridan."

"Anne Sheridan, the first-grade teacher at Pinehurst?"

"It isn't, of course, but the hair…such a gorgeous color. There aren't many people… No, what am I thinking? It couldn't be her. What would she be doing in the arms of a playboy going up to his hotel room or hers? She's not the type. All of the teachers at Pinehurst are screened carefully. Models of decorum. At least in public. No, it can't be her."

Rafik, who'd done just about every outrageous thing in the last few years in New York, felt his ears turn red. *Not the type. Not his type.* He knew that. But he'd brought her here anyway. What was wrong with him? He knew what was wrong with him. He didn't want to let her go. Didn't want to leave her anywhere. Not until he knew she was all right. On the other hand, she was a big girl. She could take care of herself. But not tonight. Tonight he was taking care of her whether she wanted him to or not. It made no sense. It made no sense at all. But there it was.

At least he should have covered Anne with something. It was one thing, as part of a colorful and wealthy international family, to be talked about in hotel lobbies. It wasn't the first time that had happened to him. But to expose Anne to gossip was not fair. He shouldn't have brought her here. He should have driven back to the reception, found out where she lived and taken her home. But hindsight is always 20/20. It was a little late to change his game plan.

He stared straight ahead, his teeth clenched in his jaw, praying for an early arrival of the elevator. After an eternity it arrived and gratefully he entered, Anne's face pressed against his chest. He awkwardly hit the button for the twentieth floor and heaved a sigh of relief. But he wasn't home free.

The elevator wasn't empty.

"Big night?" a man in a dark suit asked with a smirk.

Rafik managed a tight smile. There was no way to explain that wouldn't exacerbate the situation.

"Oh, my," said an elegant woman in a beige suit, eyeing Anne's inert body with surprise. "Is she all right?"

"Fine. She's just fine. Just tired."

"Beautiful red hair. Say, aren't you one of those sheiks?" she asked.

He'd removed his headdress this morning, but somehow the woman knew. Maybe because the family had taken over the entire twentieth floor.

"Yes," he said. "I am."

Damn. He could have lied. Could have said he was the hotel manager escorting a guest to her room or a doctor with a case of Lyme disease on his hands. How many more people was he going to run into before he got her to his floor, to his suite? He could only be glad he wasn't going to meet any family members, presumably all still at the reception. He especially wanted to avoid his father who'd had a talk with him that very morning about his new image, about public relations and the family business. This kind of situation was exactly what his father was talking about. Only it wasn't really. It just looked like it. Unfortunately his father was into appearances. In a big way.

He finally arrived in the cool, calm, quiet, high-ceilinged suite. He strode into the bedroom and laid her down on the bed on her back. Her face was pale. He sat on the edge of the bed and pressed his ear against her chest. She was breathing slowly and regularly. Thank God. Rafik knew from experience she just needed to sleep it off.

It would be just a matter of time before she came to. When she did, he'd offer her coffee and if that didn't work, he'd mix her up a concoction that worked for him—tomato juice with Worcestershire and a touch of lemon and pepper. He'd spirit her out of the hotel, down the back stairs, if there were any, and take her home. And that would be that. Carolyn would never know. She'd be on her honeymoon. All she wanted was for him to take the woman home. Which he'd tried to do. Which he would do. Eventually.

He sat on the edge of the bed observing her, his forehead furrowed. The woman in the elevator was right. She had beautiful hair. A delicious strawberry color that curled in wisps around her face. A smattering of freckles across her nose. She looked so young and innocent. She couldn't be that young. She was Carolyn's age. So she couldn't be innocent either, could she? He sighed. He knew many beautiful women with beautiful hair. Blondes, brunettes and red-heads. He'd met several today at the wedding.

But he'd never met anyone quite like this woman here on his bed. Damned if he could say what it was about her that intrigued him the way she did. Maybe it was just that she *wasn't* his type. Yes, that must be it. Opposites attract. Combine that with Carolyn's warning and it had made her damned near irresistible. He loosened his tie and looked down at her. He had an uncontrollable desire to run his fingers over her bare shoulder and down her arm to her hand that was curled up. He knew what her skin would feel like. Satin smooth. Just the way it had when he touched her this afternoon after the wedding. He fought off a shaft of desire that threatened to overtake him.

He sighed loudly, wishing she'd wake up. Wishing he could get out of this monkey suit. He imagined Anne would be more comfortable without the fancy dress she'd been wearing all day, too. After a long moment of contemplation, he rolled her gently on her side and tugged clumsily at the zipper on the back of her dress.

Carefully he pulled the dress down over her hips and tossed it on a chair. Underneath the dress she was wearing lace bikini panties and a strapless bra. He sat there staring as if he'd never seen a woman in that state before. Truth was, he'd seen many female bodies in his time. Dressed and undressed. But there was something special about this one. Something that made his heart pound. Made him short of breath. It might have been the scattering of freckles across her chest, the swell of her breasts, or the curve of her hips. She was defenseless and therefore untouchable. And oh, yes, not the most beautiful woman he'd ever seen, and definitely not his type, but very appealing, and very desirable.

This was a situation where other men might have taken

advantage of her. But there was a code of conduct he adhered to which was based on a respect for women and an obligation to help those in his care.

An obligation to make them comfortable. To protect them. He tore off his shirt, the buttons flying and covered her with it. Then he very carefully put one of her arms in the sleeve, then awkwardly the other arm. He was breathing hard from exertion. Very slowly he reached under the shirt for the strapless bra she was wearing. From experience he knew how those bras worked. Unhook the front and slip it off. But should he? What if she woke up? If she did, he'd just explain. And if she did, well, wasn't that what he wanted after all?

Under the shirt, unable to see what he was doing, he reached for the snap, but his fingers, usually so deft, felt like stubs. Finally he slid the bra off, pulled the blankets back and covered her up. She was now wearing his shirt and her panties. He'd done the best he could do.

He stood at the edge of the bed looking down at her. The red-gold hair against the white pillow. The pale face and the curve of her cheek. So sweet, so lovely. And so wrong for him. He knew that. Of course he did. As soon as he could he'd get her out of here. But when would that be? How long before she woke up? Did he dare doze off himself? All he wanted was to get her out of his bed, out of his room and out of his mind. But he couldn't. Not now. Not yet while she was still sleeping it off.

He closed the bedroom door behind him and paced back and forth in the living room, staring out the window at the lights of the city below. As tired as he was, he just couldn't go to bed. His mind was spinning. Images of the wedding filled his mind. The bride, the groom. The bridesmaid. Some time later there was a knock on the door.

"What happened to you?" his brother asked when he

opened the door. "Couldn't believe you left so early. You missed the throwing of the garter. I caught it."

"Good, that means you'll be the next to be married. And not me."

"You first," Rahman said. "You're the eldest."

"Forget it. I've heard enough of that from father. You know what happened the last time he tried to arrange a marriage for me."

"Don't blame father for that. It was nobody's fault," his brother said. "You can't give up on marriage because of one woman."

"I can't? Why not? If you feel that way, then why don't you lead the way and set an example for me," Rafik said, knowing it was a safe suggestion. Rahman was an even bigger playboy than Rafik had ever been.

"I'll give it a thought," Rahman said amiably. "Hey, aren't you going to invite me in? We can order up some coffee and rehash the wedding."

"Uh…I don't think so." Good Lord, what if the woman woke up and stumbled into the room? Not that Rahman would be shocked. Rafik just…he just didn't want his brother to think she was that kind of woman. Of course he himself didn't know what kind of woman she really was, but he could guess. She was the type to drink to cover her shyness, to make it easier to socialize.

"All right. But you still haven't explained why you left so early. I thought you and I would be rolling up the sidewalk." Leaning against the door frame, Rahman looked at his brother curiously.

"I've got to be in the office at nine tomorrow. They're installing the computer system. That's why I left early. Yeah, that's it. I can't carouse the way I used to, you know." Brilliant. That ought to satisfy his brother who knew about the increased duties his father had put on him.

Rahman observed him closely. No one knew him as well as his brother. If he could fool him, he was home free.

A soft muffled sound came from the bedroom. A sound like a sneeze.

"What was that?" Rahman asked, raising an eyebrow.

"Nothing." Damn. She hadn't made a peep since they'd arrived and she chose that moment to sneeze. Next thing he knew she'd be opening that bedroom door and…

Rahman grinned. "You've got somebody in there, haven't you? You're holding out on me. Who is it? Is it that bridesmaid I saw you with? Yeah, it's her, isn't it?"

"No, it isn't. Goodnight, Rah. Get some sleep. You need it. See you tomorrow." Very firmly and very forcefully Rafik closed the door on his brother and locked it. Then he strode across the room and flung the bedroom door open.

Chapter Two

Rafik held his breath. She was still there. Still asleep. Curled up on her side, one bare arm on the spread, her copper-colored hair still spread over the pillow, a vibrant splash of color in the soft lamplight. His heart stopped beating for a full moment, maybe longer. Good Lord, whether she was his type or not, she really was beautiful. Damn. He'd been hoping that sneeze meant she'd be up and dressed and ready to leave. Not yet.

What to do? He couldn't think straight. He was exhausted. He went into the bathroom and stripped down to his boxers. When he came out, he stood at the end of the bed debating about what to do. Watching her sleep make him feel tired and envious. Why should she get a chance to sleep in that big, comfortable bed and not him? He'd had just as hard a day as she had. Was just as tired. On the opposite side of the bed, he slid beneath the sheets and closed his eyes. Just for a few minutes.

The next thing he knew the phone was ringing. It was

his wake-up call. He jumped out of bed and did a double take. She was still there.

"Anne," he said, "wake up. It's morning."

She sighed softly. It wasn't possible for anyone to sleep through a wake-up call. She'd wake up any minute now. But he couldn't wait around until she did. He hurried into the bathroom to take a shower, then came out and dressed carefully but quickly. He couldn't be late today. From the closet he chose a London-tailored suit with a pin-striped shirt and dark tie. Then went to the living room and briskly wrote a note on his new business stationery.

"Dear Anne," he began. No, too formal. He crumpled the paper and tossed it in the wastebasket.

"Anne," he wrote. No, too brusque. Another toss in the basket.

"Hi." Yes, just the right casual tone.

Thanks for a great evening. We'll do it again some time when you're in better shape. Sorry I couldn't take you home last night but it didn't work out that way for obvious reasons. I've got things to do this morning or I'd stick around and see some more of you. I'll give you a call. Here's some taxi money.

                                    Sheik Rafik Harun.

Anne turned over when she heard a door close somewhere in the distance. She tried to open her eyes, but the sunlight that shone through the window was blinding. She pulled the sheet over her head and wondered what time it was. Though she was enjoying a summer off from teaching, she was usually up early, out in her backyard, filling her bird feeders and the birdbath. Funny. She couldn't hear the chirp of a single robin or the screech of a blue jay reminding her of her obligation to feed them and give them water.

She threw back the covers, sat up in bed and gasped. She was in a huge king-sized bed. The opposite side from hers was rumpled, covers thrown back and an indentation in the pillow. She picked it up and pressed it against her face. There was a distinct manly smell that clung to the soft cotton. What on earth? Where was she? How did she get here? Who had slept with her and, just as important, what was she wearing? It appeared to be a large man's shirt with several buttons missing. She always slept in a long flannel nightgown, suitable for the cool San Francisco summer nights. But for some inexplicable reason she had slept in someone else's shirt. And she hadn't slept alone.

She swallowed hard. Her pulse was racing. "Hello?" she called weakly. No answer. She tried again, this time louder. Silence.

Across the room her pink dress was spread across a chair. It all came back to her in a rush. The wedding. The champagne. The allergy medicine. The flirtatious sheik. But where was she? She'd obviously never made it home.

Wherever she was, she was alone. And she had a splitting headache. She was scared she couldn't remember what had happened. Even more scared she might remember.

She jumped out of bed, pressed one hand against her aching head and went to the window. She muffled a shriek. She was high above the sidewalk, looking out at the city and the San Francisco Bay. Fortunately no one could look in the window at that height, to see her in a man's white dress shirt with missing buttons, but she ought to get dressed. She found her strapless bra on the bureau and stared at it. How, where, why...and who?

She took off the shirt and buried her face in it for a brief moment. The smell was pure exotic masculinity the likes of which she'd never smelled before, and it caused her knees to tremble. The smell of the shirt reminded her of someone or something but she couldn't remember who it was. It made her head hurt more to try to remember. There were no answers to her questions. No one to ask. It was time to get dressed and get out of there. Before someone came back. The someone who'd slept next to her. The someone who belonged to the shirt.

Once she was dressed in her own clothes, she walked into the large living room, picked up the phone and pressed O for Operator.

"Front Desk."

"Yes," Anne said. "Where am I?"

"You're in room 2004 at the Stanford Arms," said a bored, uninterested voice.

"Oh, of course. Thank you." The Stanford Arms. She couldn't afford to stay at the Stanford Arms, a luxurious landmark hotel on Nob Hill. She especially couldn't afford to stay in a top-of-the-line suite there. That was when she saw the note on the table and read, the words ringing through her head:

A great evening…better shape…see more of you…taxi money…Sheik Rafik Harun.

Who on earth was that? What on earth had happened? She sat on the edge of a large overstuffed chair with her head in her hands and told herself to think. To remember. But it was so hard with her head feeling as if it were caught in a vise. Slowly, slowly it came to her. The handsome groomsman. The flirtatious sheik, driving her home. Why hadn't he? Could it be that he'd never intended to take her home? That he'd wanted to seduce her, not because she was so gorgeous or desirable, which she wasn't, but just to add another notch to his belt?

But had he? How would she know? She was a virgin. She had no idea how you felt after a night of lovemaking. She only knew that her head hurt and her whole body felt as if she'd been wrung through a wringer. Someone had removed her bra. Someone had put his shirt on her. Someone had slept next to her. That someone was a sheik. What else had he done? What had she done? The jumble of thoughts, the myriad of possibilities made her face flame. Oh, Lord, what was she going to do now? She was going to get out of there. Then she was going to find the sheik and find out what had happened last night.

She stumbled into the bathroom to wash her face. The mirror was still steamed up. The smell of soap and aftershave still in the air. She'd just missed him. Why hadn't he woken her up? Because that's the way it was. After a night of seduction, after the man got what he wanted, he left you a note saying he'd call you, left taxi money and then disappeared. Out of your life forever. Though she'd had no experience of spending the night with strange men, or any men for that matter, she knew that's how it was.

In this case he'd left his address and phone number on the stationery, as if she'd want to call him! She didn't want him to call her either. She never wanted to see him again. But she had to. She had to find out what had happened. If she could only find her shoes. And more important, her little clutch purse with her money and her house keys. They weren't under the bed and they weren't in the closet. The closet contained only men's clothes. Very expensive men's clothes. Not only suits and shirts and ties, but slacks and designer jeans and polo shirts.

She took a deep breath, picked up the phone and dialed the office number on his stationery. Her palms were damp. What would she say exactly?

How dare you take advantage of me?

Where are my shoes and my purse?

What happened anyway?

I never want to see you again!

What would he say? Would he pretend nothing happened? That he didn't know what she was talking about? She didn't get a chance to say anything because she got his voice mail and she froze. The things she thought she would say, the questions she wanted to ask, could not be spoken into a machine. They had to be spoken to a person. Sheik Rafik to be exact. She hung up.

There was only one thing to do. She'd call the house where the wedding reception had been. Perhaps the housekeeper had found her purse there.

"There was no purse here," the housekeeper said when Anne got her on the phone. "I believe you had it with you when the gentleman drove you home."

The gentleman! If only he was a gentleman. Maybe she'd left her purse and shoes in his car. She thanked the housekeeper, grabbed the money from the table and walked out the door, barefoot. She would have loved to have left the money there, but under the circumstances, she couldn't afford to. She got quite a few stares in the elevator, and even more in the lobby as she sauntered through, head held high, trying to act as if spending the night with a rich, eligible bachelor and sneaking out the next morning in the same dress happened to her every day. Why couldn't she remember coming in last night?

If only she could sneak out. But it was hard to sneak when you were barefoot, and wearing a pink bridesmaid's dress. You were bound to get a few curious glances in your direction. She got more than a few.

What a relief to get into a taxi. The driver barely gave her a second glance as she gave him Rafik's office address. Thank heavens for blasé cabdrivers. The only expression on his face was a frown when she handed him the hundred-dollar bill. He emptied his pockets and gave her change which she clutched in her hand after giving him a generous tip.

Then she stood in front of the office building on Montgomery Street in the heart of San Francisco's financial district. The pavement was cold beneath her bare feet as she stood staring up at the high-rise. Bike messengers whizzed by, horns honked, but she scarcely noticed. She wondered which office was his, wondered if she'd have the nerve to actually go up and confront him.

She had to. She had no choice. She squared her shoulders, walked through the revolving doors and strode across the marble lobby as if she belonged there. She looked straight ahead, pretending she had blinders on, ignoring whatever curious looks were directed her way, and they must have been numerous.

The office of United Venture Capitalists was on the fourteenth floor and smelled of fresh paint and new carpets. A well-groomed receptionist behind a cherrywood desk first greeted her with a smile then her mouth fell open in surprise as she took in Anne's unusual and unbusiness-like appearance.

"My name is Anne Sheridan. I'm here to see Sheik Rafik Harun," Anne said, summoning all the dignity she had.

"Uh…yes. Do you have an appointment?" the receptionist asked. As if a barefoot woman in a formal dress *would* have an appointment with a sheik.

"No, but I have to see him."

"I'll see if he's in," she said coolly. "Won't you sit down?"

Anne was too nervous to sit down. Instead she stood looking at the pictures on the wall of the ventures the company had funded. She examined a portrait of the grandfather who'd founded the company, a distinguished-looking sheik in traditional Arab dress. When she heard male voices approaching, she whirled around. It was not Rafik. It was an older man who looked very much like the sheik in the picture on the wall with an American who was wearing jeans and a T-shirt.

"May I help you, my dear?" the older man asked with a slight bow.

She swallowed hard. "I'm here to see Rafik."

His gaze flicked over her dress. He pressed his lips together in a tight line. He seemed to understand without asking, just what had happened. Though he couldn't possibly know when she didn't even know herself. Unless it was a common occurrence for women to appear in evening gowns unannounced, asking for his son. She wouldn't be surprised.

"I see," he said. "Where is my elder son?" he asked the receptionist.

Her gaze fluttered from her desk to her telephone to the elder sheik. "I...I believe he's in his office."

"Then show the young lady in," he ordered.

"Yes, sir, right away." She jumped up from her desk and while the two men watched she led Anne down the hall to the large office on the corner. She knocked on the door and when Rafik yelled for her to come in, the woman opened the door, ushered Anne in and then disappeared.

Rafik was seated behind an enormous desk talking on the phone with his back to the door and to Anne. She had an excellent view of the back of his handsome head and his broad shoulders in his well-tailored suit jacket. Her heart was hammering in her chest like a tom-tom. This was a terrible idea. She should just turn around and walk out while she still could. He'd never know. But his father would tell him. And she still didn't have her purse.

"Yes, of course I'll be there," he said. "The whole family will be there and very pleased to be hosting the benefit

this year.... It gives us a chance to meet the community....
No, not yet. I'm new in town, you know. Haven't had a
chance to meet many women...." That was the only reason
he'd spent the night with her, Anne thought. He didn't
know any other women. He chuckled, and Anne shivered.
If only she had a jacket, a coat, a sweater. Anything. But
no sweater would prevent the chill that his words sent
through her. If she left now, he'd never know she was ever
there. But she couldn't. Even if she'd wanted to. Her feet
were made of lead. She couldn't move a muscle.

"A woman in my hotel room?" Rafik asked, sounding
shocked at the very idea. Anne wished she could sink into
the Oriental carpet and disappear. "You must have me confused with someone else," he said genially. "I know how
important the social column is," he continued, "but I'm
afraid I can't help you there. I can't imagine who the
woman was, but I know she wasn't with me. I realize I've
had an image as a swinging bachelor, but all that's in the
past. From now on I'll have no more time for partying.
Well," he said, "it's been a pleasure to talk to you. I can't
emphasize enough that the whole family is very serious
about being a part of this beautiful city. Both the business
community and the social scene and the local charities. We
want to do our part." He hung up and spun his chair around
to face her.

Anne swallowed hard. She'd forgotten how handsome
he was. So handsome in his dark suit and bronzed skin
against his striped shirt that she almost fainted. Of course,
that feeling could also come from hunger or shame. She
wrapped her arms across her waist.

"Oh," he said, standing and stuffing his hands in his
pockets. If he was surprised to see her, he didn't show it.
Neither did he show pleasure or dismay at her appearance.
Of course, sheiks were probably trained to handle situations

like this. Smoothly, suavely, with savoir faire. "It's good to see you again...Anne."

He remembered her name. That was a good start.

"What happened last night?" she blurted.

"Happened? As in between you and me?"

"Yes, exactly."

"Well, you passed out," he said matter-of-factly. "A little too much champagne. It can happen to anyone. It's happened to me. Nothing to worry about."

"Nothing to worry about? I was in your car. You were taking me home. Why didn't you?"

"I tried, believe me, I tried. But I didn't know where you lived, and you were in no condition to tell me."

"So you took me to your hotel," she said.

"Right," he said. "I had no choice. Then you fell asleep in my bed. End of story."

"That's it? That's all?" How desperately she wanted to believe that. "Wait a minute. How did I get my dress off and your shirt on?"

He raised his right hand. "Guilty as charged. Only because you looked so uncomfortable. I thought you'd sleep better in my shirt." He walked around his desk and gave her a long, lingering look, trying but not succeeding to conceal the smile on his face. "Yes, you looked much more...how shall I say, comfortable, in my shirt. You'll be glad to know I averted my eyes at all the appropriate moments. As any gentleman would."

"Any gentleman would have woken me up."

He shook his head. "I tried, darling, believe me, I tried. You were out cold. Don't tell me it's never happened to you before?"

"No, it hasn't. But I imagine it's happened to you. Taking a woman back to your hotel and then...and then..."

"Yes, it has. A time or two. But last night was different."

"Really." What did that mean?

He smiled. "Definitely."

"Maybe you think this is funny," she fumed, running out of patience. "To be stuck in a hotel without your shoes or your purse." *Not to know if you'd made love to a total stranger.* "But I don't."

"No, of course not," he said. "Here's what happened. I took your shoes off in my car. And I saw your bare feet. You can't object too strongly since everyone else you've run into today probably enjoyed the same pleasure."

"I'm not worried about people seeing my feet. It's my…it's the rest of my…you know."

"I can assure you no one saw but me. No one knows but me. No one will know for sure what really happened. Some may have doubts, like my father and my brother who are both suspicious types. But I won't tell if you don't tell."

"How can I tell when I don't know?"

"You'll just have to trust me."

Trust him? Trust a Middle Eastern sheik whom she didn't even know? Not likely.

"I need my shoes and my purse," she said.

"They must be in my car. I forgot completely. I'll send someone to get them right away." He picked up the phone and gave the order. Then he turned back to her. "Why don't you sit down and make yourself comfortable? It will only take a few minutes. In the meantime, take my jacket. You look…" he shot her a swift appraising look "…cold." He went to a closet and removed a soft, cashmere suit jacket and put it around her shoulders. His fingertips grazed her bare shoulders. It all came back to her. The wedding, her tears, his touch. Her face grew hot. She thrust her arms stiffly into the sleeves of the jacket.

"I'll stand," she said. Though she didn't know how long her legs would hold her up, she had her pride. He shrugged. There was a long silence. He leaned against his desk and his gaze locked with hers. Those eyes, those deep, dark eyes a woman could get lost in. A woman could forget why she was there, forget the questions she'd come to ask. Especially a woman with no experience in matters like this.

In a few minutes someone would appear with her shoes and her keys and she'd leave, never to see him again. If she didn't ask now, she'd never know.

She took a deep breath and gathered her wits about her. "What really did happen in your hotel room?"

He didn't answer for a long moment. She could almost sense the indecision that hovered in his mind. Something flickered in his dark eyes. Then he spoke. "You and I had the most incredible night of our lives. At least I did. I can't speak for you."

Before her knees collapsed under her, Anne sank into the leather chair next to his desk, the one she'd spurned a few minutes ago, and buried her head in her hands. "I don't believe it," she said in a muffled tone.

"Why not? Am I that unattractive? Do I repulse you?" he asked.

She peeked at him between her fingers. No, he didn't repulse her. In fact, he was the most attractive man she'd ever met. The thought of him making love to her raised the temperature of her whole body about ten degrees. Surely he knew how handsome he was. He was teasing her.

"Of course not," she said. "If it was the most incredible night of my life, I wish I could remember it."

"All I can say is we'll have to do it again," he said, a smile playing at the corner of his mouth. "When you're in better shape."

"Wait a minute. You think I was drunk, don't you? I

wasn't. I'd taken a strong antihistamine for my allergies and that combined with two glasses of champagne did me in. Not that it matters. I just didn't want you to think I was the kind of person who drinks too much and passes out in some stranger's bed.''

"You're not?" he asked, a spark of laughter in his eyes. "That's too bad."

Anne opened her mouth to retort, but no sound came out. She had no practice in bantering with sexy men. He was an expert in lighthearted repartee. She wasn't. He wasn't serious. But what if he was? What if she'd made love to a perfect stranger? She knew for sure they'd shared a bed. Anything could have happened. But did it? Would she ever get a straight answer from him?

Fortunately, Rafik's phone rang and he began another conversation, as if she weren't there at all, sparing her the effort of trying to pin him down and him the effort of continuing to evade her questions. She crossed and uncrossed her legs. She squirmed and wiggled. It was a comfortable chair but she was far from comfortable. It was that awful dress. At one time she'd thought it beautiful. She'd helped Carolyn pick them out and agreed that they were not only becoming, but could be worn again, to the kind of party Anne never went to. But never mind about that.

The dress made her skin itch and squeezed her waist. But the jacket was wonderfully warm and smelled like him. Like leather and exotic soap. How did she know what he smelled like? That was a good question. But not *the* question. Had they been intimate?

When was the person coming with her purse and shoes so she could get out of there? Rafik didn't want her there, and she didn't want to be there. There was a knock on the door. Rafik hung up. She got to her feet. At last. But it was not her shoes and purse. It was his father.

"May I present my father, Sheik Massoud Harun."

Anne murmured something polite.

"Who, may I ask, son, is this lovely lady? She looks familiar, but I can't quite place her. You must forgive an old man, my dear, but my memory is not what it used to be."

"This is Anne...Anne Sheridan," Rafik said. "You met her at the wedding yesterday, Father. She was one of the bridesmaids."

"Ah, yes, of course. How nice to see you again."

Anne murmured something polite. It was too bad Rafik didn't have half the charm his father did. Maybe some day, years from now, he'd acquire it. But she wouldn't be around to see it. If the old man thought her apparel strange or wondered why she was there, dressed as she was in a dress and his son's jacket, he gave no indication at all. Or else he was past wondering at his son's exploits.

"Well, I won't interrupt you two young people any longer," Rafik's father said. "I imagine you have a lot to talk about. Don't forget to invite her to our gala benefit this month, Rafik. Since we're new in town, we want to expand our circle of acquaintances. Beautiful female acquaintances especially."

Rafik stared at his father with surprise. Not a happy surprise. He recovered quickly. "Consider it done," he said swiftly. "Ms. Sheridan is on our guest list. It will be delightful to see her again."

His father left the room wearing a satisfied smile, his mission obviously accomplished.

"Don't worry," Anne said as soon as the door closed behind him. "I have no wish to go to any gala benefit. I've had enough fancy parties this month to last me a lifetime."

"I understand completely," Rafik said, feeling a giant surge of relief. "I'll convey your regrets to my father."

Anne Sheridan would have been totally out of place at this party. Ostensibly a benefit for a charity, it was really a thinly veiled device for his father to find a bride for him. Not Rahman, just him. It wasn't fair. Thirty minutes seniority and his father's focus was on him. While Rahman played the field, played golf whenever he wanted to, and came to work whenever he felt like it, Rafik was expected to take over the investments of a huge family corporation.

He agreed it was time to get to work, he welcomed the chance to put his stamp on the family investments, but he didn't agree it was time to get married. His plan was to reject all the women as unsuitable no matter what his father said or how impeccable their credentials. He didn't know if it would work, but he'd give it a try because there was no way in hell he was going to get married. He'd tried that. He'd gone so far as to get engaged. It hadn't worked. His father knew it, but he hadn't given up. Not yet.

A few minutes later, the messenger knocked on the door, handed Anne her purse and shoes then closed the door behind him.

"My driver will take you home," Rafik said. "He'll be waiting at the front entrance." He took her by the hand and leaned over to give her a perfunctory kiss on the cheek. But she turned her face at the last moment and their lips met. Just a brush of her lips, and he felt as if he was falling down a slippery slope. He couldn't stop himself. Operating on pure instinct, he put one hand on her shoulder, the other cradled the back of her head and he deepened the kiss. He felt her gasp of surprise, felt her try to back off, then sigh and give in. She didn't kiss him back, but neither did she pull away. She could have. He wasn't holding her that tightly. Frankly he was shocked at his reaction. An ordinary kiss had caused a surge of desire to course through his veins. What the hell was wrong with him?

When he came to his senses and dropped his hands he saw she had turned several shades of pink brighter than her dress. "How dare you," she said.

"How dare I? After what we've been through together? That was nothing." It *was* nothing. Just a kiss. But what a kiss. Didn't she feel it, too?

"Nothing?" She spun on her bare heels and headed for the door. But before she left, she raised her arm and threw a handful of dollar bills across the room. "There. That's the change from your hundred dollars. I'll send you a check for what I owe you for the cab fare."

"Come on, Anne, I don't want your money."

"And I don't want yours. I never want to see you again."

"Wait a minute." He couldn't let her leave like this, thinking he'd seduced her. It was a matter of pride. "Nothing happened last night. I mean it. I was teasing you."

"Nothing?" she said again.

Solemnly, he shook his head.

She gave him a long look, then she shook her head, walked out the door and slammed it behind her. Rafik collapsed into the same chair she'd been sitting in. Which was where his brother found him ten minutes later.

Rahman sat on the edge of Rafik's desk and observed his brother with a mixture of humor and complacence. "So you got caught, did you?"

"I don't know," Rafik said. "Did I?"

"Father thinks so. Of course I told him nothing of what I knew."

"That's because you know nothing."

"So you say," Rahman said. "I know she was with you last night and I know she was here today. The woman in pink. Still wearing the same dress as yesterday. How can you deny something happened between you?"

Rafik sighed loudly. "Why should I bother? No one believes me. In any case, she's history."

"That's not what I heard. Father says she's coming to the party," Rahman said.

"He invited her but she won't come. Not her kind of thing. She's really not the party animal you think."

"It doesn't matter what I think. What do you think?" Rahman asked.

"I don't think. I just did what I had to do. Can we forget the woman for a moment? I told you she's history. She doesn't want to see me again and I don't want to see her."

"A one-night stand."

"Yes. Whatever." Rafik didn't want to see Anne, think about her, talk about her or examine his unexpected reaction to that strange kiss. "I have bigger problems. The biggest being this damned scheme of Father's to find me a bride. What am I going to do? How am I going to put him off?"

"What you need is a decoy. How do they call it? A beard."

"What's that?" Rafik asked. Sometimes his brother was amazing. Often when he'd discounted him as a hopeless hedonist, he'd come up with a brilliant idea. He hoped this was one of those times.

"You find a woman who will pretend to be your girlfriend, fiancée, whatever it takes to pacify Father, then he'll stop looking," Rahman said.

"But I don't know anyone like that. I'm new in town as are you. We don't know any women we can ask such a favor of."

"We don't?" Rahman asked. "Are you sure?"

"Sure. Absolutely sure."

"What about that woman you spent the night with last night. What's wrong with her?"

"Wrong with her? Everything. No, absolutely not. Didn't you hear me tell you she didn't ever want to see me again?"

"When has that ever stopped you from pursuing a woman? Usually you like a challenge."

"Anne Sheridan is more than a challenge. She's a stone wall." But kissing her was not like kissing a stone wall. It was more like kissing flower petals. The memory caused a wave of sensual awareness to rocket through his body.

"We'll buy her off. Even a stone wall has a price. We'll offer her money to play the part. She can't refuse," Rahman suggested.

"Hah. You see this money all over the floor? She threw it there. Does that sound like a woman who can be bought? No, your plan won't work. Besides…"

"Besides what? You're afraid to get entangled with her, aren't you? You have feelings for her. I knew it last night. You can't fool me. Don't even try. I'm your twin. I know what you're thinking."

"Not this time," Rafik said, glaring at his brother. It was true. The twins didn't often have secrets from each other. But this was one secret Rafik was determined to keep. He didn't want his brother interfering with him and this woman. Though there was really nothing to interfere with. It was over. He wasn't going to see her again.

"Then prove it. Offer her something in return. Something she wants. Everybody wants something. So she threw your money at you. Maybe she was angry," Rahman suggested.

"Maybe? You know what they say about redheads. You should have seen her. There were sparks coming from her eyes. She was breathing fire."

Rahman chuckled. "Sounds like your type. She's quite a woman. Looks good in your jacket, too. I saw her on her way out. Okay, you say you're not interested? No feelings? Then you won't mind if I give her a call?''

Rafik jumped up from his chair and grabbed his brother by the collar of his shirt. "Don't even think about it."

"I'll think about it. Unless you do something. Go see her. Ask her. I dare you."

When had Rafik ever refused a dare? Especially from his brother? It was like showing a red cape to a bull.

Chapter Three

A few days later Anne was still trying desperately to forget the unpleasant and disturbing encounter she had had with the sheik in his office. First there was the humiliating journey from the hotel to downtown. And then their face-to-face meeting. It was not like her to lose her temper and throw things like money or to slam doors. But he'd asked for it. Teasing her about what had happened the night before. Which story was she supposed to believe? She wanted to think that nothing had happened. So she resolved to accept that story. Fine. But what really bothered her was the kiss. No, not the kiss. That was to be expected from a playboy sheik.

It was her reaction to the kiss that shocked her. She was ashamed to admit how much she'd liked it. She was disturbed at what an effect it had on her. All the way home in his chauffeured car she'd felt her lips tingle and her heart pound. As usual, she took refuge in the backyard of the small house her parents had helped her buy on a quiet street in the Sunset district of San Francisco.

She'd spent the last few days planting and replanting shrubs and bushes and pruning her raspberry plants, part of a grand plan to turn a small plot of earth into a minor bird sanctuary of her own. She had a whole summer ahead of her, but she'd set a timetable for herself. Her friends teased her about being overly organized, but she liked to know what she was doing and when. She had goals and deadlines, even in the summer. When she had it finished she was going to host a meeting of bird-watchers. She looked forward to sharing the fruits of her work with those who would truly appreciate it. Not only the birds, but her fellow bird lovers.

She was planting a small oak sapling when she heard someone call her name from the side of her house. She wiped her dirty hands on her overalls, went to the wooden gate and peered over it.

It was him. She rocked back on her heels, speechless with surprise. How had he found out where she lived? He looked just the same as the last time she'd seen him. Except he was lacking his suit jacket in keeping with the informality of her informal abode. Otherwise he was perfectly groomed in a tailored shirt that looked as though it had been made for him, carefully creased slacks, a subdued tie and polished wing-tip shoes. Every dark hair was combed in place except for a strand that fell across his forehead. Then it came to her; she realized why he was there.

"I'm terribly sorry," she said.

"I thought you would be," he said from the other side of the fence. "When you'd had a chance to think it over."

"What?"

"I knew you were going to apologize for throwing my money at me. Can I come in?" he asked.

She wanted to say no. She wanted him to disappear. If that wasn't possible she wished she could disappear. She also wished she'd just hidden and pretended no one was at home. But unfortunately it was too late to do anything of the sort. Instead, she reached up and unlatched the gate. And suddenly he was in her garden. He had intruded on her own personal haven. She sighed loudly. It was her own fault.

"Stay right here," she said. "I'll get it."

"Get what?" he asked.

"Your jacket. Isn't that why you're here?"

"No." He stood there a moment, between her lavender plants in all their purple glory and her birdbath and her small raised vegetable garden. His gaze traveled from her unruly hair brushing her shoulders to her dirt-stained overalls and the skimpy white T-shirt underneath. His eyes also took in her flip-flops and her dusty toes. "What are you doing?" he asked, his forehead furrowed.

"I'm planting a tanbark oak sapling. The redheaded woodpeckers will love the acorns. Of course that stage is a long way off, but in the meantime the junipers and the cedars I put in give shelter and nesting sites and…" She stopped before she got carried away. He looked interested, his gaze didn't waver, but after all, what did he care about her provisions for migratory and local birds? "I might ask you the same thing," she said. "What are *you* doing? If you didn't come for your jacket, why did you come?"

"Yes, good question. Can we sit down somewhere?" he asked, looking around the garden. She had to admit he didn't look quite as sure of himself, quite as arrogant as he did in his office. She almost smiled to see him look just a little anxious, perhaps a trifle unsure of himself after their last meeting. Now they were on her turf. Whatever he wanted with her, he wasn't sure he was going to get it. Unless it was just his jacket.

She motioned grandly to a wrought-iron bench which he

sat on. She pulled up a small wooden stool she used to reach the top branches of her crabapple tree and sat down to face him.

"I apologize for not calling first. Actually I did call first," he explained, "but no one answered. Carolyn's mother was kind enough to give me your address. I hope you don't mind."

"Actually it will save me a trip to the post office. I was going to send your jacket back. Why don't I run upstairs and get it?" She stood up. He got up and put his hand on her arm.

"First I need to ask you something."

She shrugged and sat down again.

He sat down and looked around. "I thought you had allergies. How do you manage to have a garden?"

She was sure that wasn't the question he'd come all this way to ask, but she answered it anyway. "I'm only allergic to flowers. I didn't find out until I had skin tests done last year and when I got the results I had to replant. As you can see I don't have any flowers in the garden now and I'm fine."

"I see. It's very beautiful. Who takes care of it for you?" he asked.

"I do," she said. "As you see. Does that surprise you?"

"A little. Where I come from women don't like to get their hands dirty. So they hire a gardener."

"I can't afford a gardener, and even if I could, I think I'd do it myself. I have gloves, but I confess I like the feel of the dirt between my fingers. It's very therapeutic, getting your hands dirty." She looked down at her feet. "And your toes, too."

"Therapeutic, you say. Is there some reason you need therapy?" The question seemed innocent enough, but there was a gleam in his eyes that indicated he was teasing her again.

She felt her cheeks flush. It hadn't taken long for him to assume his former personality. The one that liked to tease and annoy her so much. The one that liked to pry into her personal life just to see how far he could push her. She got up off her wooden stool and stood looking at him.

"Everyone needs therapy some time. This is the kind that doesn't cost a penny and doesn't require any professional help. I assume you are the exception to the rule. A person who needs nothing. So if you didn't come for your jacket and you don't need anything, why are you here?"

"Ah, yes. That. I am here to ask you to reconsider your decision not to attend our gala ball."

"You drove all the way out here from your office to ask me that?"

"I told you I tried to call."

"The answer is still no."

"There's more," he said as if he hadn't heard her turn him down.

She opened her mouth to say she didn't want to hear any more, but he continued before she could speak.

"I need a fiancée."

She was astonished at his brashness. What did that have to do with her? Why should she care if he needed a fiancée or even a white elephant, for that matter? "Good luck," she said.

He gave her a rueful smile. "You think I'll have trouble finding one."

"In a word, yes."

"Some women find me charming," he said.

"Then ask one of them. Now I'll get your jacket."

"Wait. Please. I don't mean a real fiancée. Though that's what my father, Massoud, whom you met the other day, wants for me. I'm thirty-one and he thinks I should get married and settle down. For many reasons too numerous to go into right now, I am against this plan."

"Why get married when there are so many willing women around?" she asked.

His eyes narrowed for a moment and then he smiled. "Exactly. Then you heard. What I'm looking for is not a real fiancée but someone who's willing to pose as one for a short time. A very short time. Maybe just one evening."

"So what's the problem? Ask one of those willing women to pose for you. How could they say no to a charming man like you?" Anne was proud of herself for coming up with a suitable reply. Charming? He was just too full of himself, this handsome sheik.

Rafik gave her a quick, admiring glance and held one finger in the air. "Touché," he said. "I deserve that. Actually I haven't asked anyone yet. Since I'm new in town I don't know many women. And so…"

His gaze drifted around the garden, lingering on the birdhouse hanging from the eaves of her house. She tried to wait patiently, but she was running out of patience. She had weeds to pull and shrubs to plant. His presence made her uneasy. Maybe it was the memory of their last meeting. That kiss she had tried so hard to forget. She plucked a few dead leaves off the low branches of her apple tree.

"I thought perhaps you…" he continued.

"Me?" Her eyes widened in surprise. "You thought I would pose as your fiancée? Why would I do that?"

"Obviously not on account of my charm," he said ruefully.

"Obviously," she said.

"Perhaps there's something you need, something you want. A gardener… No, you don't want a gardener. You prefer to feel the dirt between your fingers, isn't that right?''

"That's right. I have everything I need.'' So he thought he could buy her the way he bought everything else he wanted. Of course, she didn't have everything she needed or wanted. A small pond, a recycling water supply and sprinklers for the garden were things she would love to have eventually. Also her bird-watching club was raising money to buy the marshland south of the city for a preserve, but that had nothing to do with him.

"All right," he said. "I hope you don't think I was trying to bribe you."

"Not at all," she said calmly. "Before you go, let me get your…"

"There is just one thing," he said getting to his feet.

She paused.

"I thought after reflecting on that night we spent together, the hours we shared…you might feel differently about me," he said. "You might want to help me out."

She stared at him. "That night we spent together, according to you, nothing happened. That's what you said. Nothing happened."

"I didn't want to upset you."

"Well you have upset me. I want to know the truth."

"Ah, the truth. What is the truth after all? All I can say is that it was…"

"The most incredible night of your life. I know. You said that before. Before you said nothing happened. I will not come to your gala and I will most definitely not pretend to be your fiancée. Now, if you'll excuse me, I have a lot of work to do."

He nodded. But he didn't look as chastened or discouraged as she'd hoped. He broke off a sprig of lavender and stuck it in his shirt pocket. Then he gave her a brief smile and left the same way he came. Anne stood in the middle of the garden staring at the gate. Remembering that she'd forgotten to give him his jacket. Pleased and proud of herself for standing her ground. For not giving in. For not admitting even to herself that the man had entirely too much charm for his own good. Good luck to him in finding a woman to pose as his fiancée. She sat down with a thud on the bench just vacated by him and let out a large breath of air she didn't know she was holding.

Somehow she knew this garden would never feel the same to her. Though he was gone, it was almost as if he was still there. She felt his presence as if he were still sitting on this bench. His golden-brown skin contrasting with his white shirt and his teeth. His dark eyes always laughing at her. Always teasing her. *The night we spent together, the hours we shared....* He almost had her believing that something did happen that night. That was his intent. To make her worry and make her wonder. Well, it wasn't going to work. She broke off a sprig of lavender as he'd done and the perfume filled the air. She was afraid she'd always think of him when she smelled lavender in the air. Damn, damn, damn.

Rafik stopped in front of her house for a brief moment before he went to his car. It was a small, modest house with similar two-story stucco houses on either side. He imagined that hers was the only one with an amazing garden that she apparently had planted herself. No flowers, which he remembered she was allergic to, just aromatic bushes and trees and a vegetable plot arranged in a way that made a pleasing impression and would have practical benefits. The whole thing mirrored his impression of Anne. A practical girl, but decorative as well. Yes, very decorative.

Like Anne, there was more to the garden than met the eye at first glance. The longer he sat there on her bench, the more aware he was of the garden's hidden charms, like the purple cabbage planted in a concentric circle around artichoke plants. As for Anne's hidden charms...he had become more aware of her high spirits, her pride in her garden and of course of her physical attributes hinted at by her overalls and skimpy T-shirt.

He removed the lavender sprig from his pocket and crushed it between his fingers, releasing the most wonderful fragrance. As spicy and piquant as Anne was herself. Shy on the outside, she had a spirit that was far from shy. When aroused, she was downright fiery. He could only imagine what kind of a lover she'd be. Not that he would ever find out. She'd made it quite clear how she felt about him. She couldn't stop him from dreaming, however. Or stop him from thinking about her soft skin with the smattering of freckles across her chest. Or wondering how it would feel if he tangled his fingers in her red-gold hair.

Seeing her in those dungarees and T-shirt had surprised him. She looked even more desirable than in her pink dress. Another surprise. She didn't seem fazed by having a guest see her like that. He didn't know any women who wouldn't have run inside to change their clothes at the sight of a caller at the door. Or who liked feeling the dirt between their fingers.

How different she was from his former fiancée, the one his family had chosen for him. She had appeared to be the perfect choice. *Perfect* was the word for her. Perfect ease in social situations, perfect clothes and hair, perfect manners. Until he discovered she was only interested in his money and position. The breakup led him to his decision never to marry. Never to trust another woman. His parents, on the other hand, had not lost faith. They had become even more determined to find him another bride. This one would be better, they assured him. This one would be the right one. They'd been trying to find her ever since. Determined to see him settled down, in the job and in his personal life as well. Fortunately, as for a wife, they hadn't yet had any luck.

As he drove back to his office Rafik was only slightly discouraged. Maybe he should be more so. Anne certainly hadn't given him any encouragement. In fact, she'd been just as spirited in her refusal as she'd been when she refused to accept any money from him and had thrown it across the floor. He smiled at the memory. Her flushed cheeks, her flashing eyes, her disheveled hair. And at the memory of that kiss they'd shared. He wondered if she remembered it. He didn't know what he'd do next. He only knew he wasn't giving up. He was determined to see her again. To persuade her at least to come to the gala if not to pose as his fiancée.

Pinehurst School was a wonderful place to teach and to learn. The classes were small, the students were all above average and the campus was beautiful. Teachers were dedicated and respected. The school was located on the grounds of a mansion once owned by a San Francisco millionaire. For fifty years it had been a private school for the children of the well-to-do in Pacific Heights, a neighborhood that enjoyed spectacular views of the Bay and the Golden Gate Bridge.

It was now summer vacation for the children, though some took advantage of the summer enrichment program. The headmistress was in her office when she telephoned Anne that week and asked her to stop by for a moment when she had time.

As Anne walked through the leafy campus, hearing the

shouts of the small soccer players as they ran up and down the field, she wasn't worried. But she was curious. She'd turned in her student evaluations the week before, taken down the posters on the walls so her classroom could be painted over the vacation and in general had left things pretty shipshape. At least she thought so.

"Come in and sit down," Leona Feathergill said to Anne. "I hope you're having a pleasant summer?"

"Yes, lovely," Anne said, feeling a small tremor of anxiety somewhere between her shoulder blades. Now she knew what it must be like for her students when summoned to the headmistress's office. Leona could be stern, but she was usually fair also. What on earth was this all about? Surely she hadn't been called into the office to talk about her summer vacation. "I've been doing quite a bit of work in my garden and bird-watching," she added.

"Is that all?" Leona asked.

Anne gave a little shrug which she hoped could mean almost anything. She wanted to ask what she should be doing? She had no idea what the woman was getting at.

Leona nodded absently and shuffled some papers on her desk. She almost seemed more nervous than Anne. She cleared her throat.

"You've always been one of our most outstanding teachers," Leona said. "I hear nothing but praise from both the students and their parents for you."

"Thank you," Anne said. Now she was getting worried. This sounded like the top of the sandwich from one of those books on how to succeed, how to manage a staff and get along with your colleagues and underlings. The strategy was to use first the praise on top, then the criticism in the middle and then finish off the bottom layer with some more praise. How she wished the woman would get on with it.

"I had a call from one of the parents the other day. Actually from more than one."

"Oh?"

"It seems they saw you in a compromising position in a hotel downtown. I hardly knew what to say."

Anne's heart sank. How long would the memory of that infamous night continue to haunt her? "I think I know what you're referring to," she said quickly. But she didn't. Were they referring to the morning when she tiptoed through the lobby or the evening, which was a blank in her memory. Her mind was spinning. What to say. How to explain.

"I never pry into any of my teachers' private lives," Leona continued. "And yet when it affects their reputations and that of the school, I feel I should give them a chance to respond."

"Yes, of course." Anne was stalling for time.

"It involved a man. Of course I know you aren't married and you have a perfect right to have dates, er...relationships, whatever. It's just that the parents who saw you reported that this was in a very public place and that you were in a very compromising position."

Anne knew only one thing. If it involved a man, they must be referring to the evening. She wondered just what they'd seen. Since she'd been unconscious at the time, she wasn't sure. What did a *compromising position* mean exactly? She realized she couldn't ask that. Leona was waiting. She had to say something.

"I think I can explain," she said, pressing her palms together.

"Good. I assume the man was someone you are well acquainted with," Leona said. "Since he carried you across the lobby and up to his room."

"Oh, yes," she said. "Of course." *Across the lobby and up to his room? How many people saw her?* "You see, I'd been to a wedding reception where I was the bridesmaid. I was feeling ill so my...my fiancé brought me back to the hotel where the wedding party was staying.''

"You included.''

"That's right," Anne said gratefully. "We were all staying there.''

Then why were you still wearing your pink bridesmaid dress the next morning? she imagined Leona asking. But thankfully, she didn't. Maybe no one she knew saw her in the morning. She could only hope.

Leona appeared to relax. She even smiled. "I didn't know you were engaged, Anne. Congratulations.''

"Thank you.'' She didn't know it herself, she thought. It had just popped into her mind. She knew why. It was all that talk about a faux fiancée. If he could get one, so could she. She'd had no idea if a fiancé would make a difference until she saw the relief on Leona's face. Then she knew she'd said the right thing and her impulse had been correct. "I know it must have looked scandalous," Anne continued. "But it was all quite innocent." But was it? Would she ever find out the truth? Only one person knew what had happened that night, and he was not to be believed. For her own peace of mind she decided to accept his version of what happened. And that was that nothing happened.

"And quite romantic," Leona said.

In lieu of a response, Anne forced a smile. She'd run out of lies and excuses. She just wanted to get out of the office and back to her real life. A life out of the spotlight. A life without sheiks and their problems. Without fancy clothes and chauffeur-driven cars. A life without tension. Without lies. Assuming the interview was over, Anne stood up.

"I'd like to meet him," Leona said. "And so would the rest of the staff. After all, it isn't every day one of our teachers gets engaged to a sheik.''

Anne's heart skipped a beat. She licked her lips. She tried to say something but no words came out. If she could have spoken she would have said, *Who said he was a sheik? What makes you think I am engaged to a sheik?*

As if she'd heard Anne's silent questions, Leona casually mentioned that the parents who'd seen her in the hotel were aware of the buzz in the lobby. The questions, the gossip, the interest in finding out who was the woman the sheik was with.

"It would be my pleasure to have a little get-together as we did for Marcia last spring when she got engaged," Leona said as she reached for her calendar. "After all, we like to think we're one big happy family here at Pinehurst."

Anne stood still as a statue. Inside a voice was shouting *no no no. No get-together. No engagement. No sheik.* But there was silence in the room as Leona perused her calendar. "What about a week from Saturday in the Hall?" she asked.

"I...I...I'll have to..." Anne stammered.

"Of course you'll have to check with your fiancé, the sheik." She smiled. "My sources reported that he's quite handsome."

And rich, Anne wanted to add. *And arrogant.* Haven't your sources reported that yet?

Somehow she managed to leave the office and walk through the campus to the parking lot without running into any students or other teachers. She tried to replay the conversation to figure out how on earth she'd gotten herself into this fix. She tried to think of how she could have avoided it, and lastly she tried to think of a way to get out of it. But her brain refused to cooperate. Once in her car, she rested her head against the steering wheel. She tried to blink back the tears of frustration, but they fell against the leather.

All afternoon she told herself to get it over with. She had to call him. Tell him she'd go to the gala. That's all. Take the first step. See how it went. If she couldn't abide his manners, his authoritarian way, his so-called charm, she'd go back to the school, tell Leona it was all a misunderstanding. She wasn't engaged. That wasn't even her in that compromising position. It must have been someone else. The way she had it worked out in her mind, it all made sense. Then why did she dread making that call? She wasn't afraid of him. Especially when he wasn't occupying the same space as she was.

In the back of her mind it occurred to her that maybe he wasn't so bad. Maybe she'd gone overboard in thinking badly of him. Maybe she could tolerate him for an evening at his gala in return for his pretending to be her fiancé for a short reception. Then when school began in the fall her colleagues might have forgotten about her so-called engagement.

Forget about an engagement to a sheik? Probably not. But she'd worry about that later. There were months left to summer vacation, months left to come up with an explanation. All she needed to do was to call him. That shouldn't be so hard.

She could deal with a disembodied voice on the phone. She had a harder time when he was right there in her garden or in his office. Where she was only too aware of the way he looked at her, as if he was going to eat her up. Aware too of the tension in the air, the force of his personality that caused her to come up with answers, to match him word for word. She could feel herself changing when she was around him. Becoming more sure of herself, more confident and yes…more feminine, more desirable. That part wasn't bad. The part that scared her was that she didn't know what he'd do next. He didn't seem to get the message that she was not interested in having anything more to do with him. Now that she knew nothing had happened that night, he could forget about her and she could forget about him. Then why did she keep thinking about him? Why did she wonder what he was going to do next?

Rafik was about to go into a meeting with his father and his brother. Before he went into Massoud's office, he paused at the secretary's desk. "If I get a call from an Anne Sheridan, please let me know. It's important."

When he looked up he saw his brother leaning against the door and listening to every word he'd said. Rahman raised an eyebrow. Together they walked into their father's office to wait for the old sheik.

"What happened?" Rahman asked.

"Nothing," Rafik said. He hated to admit defeat.

"Did you ask her?"

"I asked her. She said no," Rafik said.

"But you expect her to call you and change her mind, according to what I just heard you say to Ruth. After all, how many women have turned you down? I'd say zero, just offhand."

"This is different. I've never asked anybody to pretend to be my fiancée before," he said with a quick glance around as if his father might be hiding somewhere behind a bookcase.

"But why? Why wouldn't she go for it?" Rahman asked.

"I guess I didn't make a very good case for it. Don't worry. I haven't given up."

"That's my brother. Never give up. Never surrender."

"I won't. Especially when I think of the alternative to choosing my own fiancée. My own *temporary* fiancée," he added quickly. "There's no way I'd want a real one. Father's idea of someone suitable is miles away from my idea. She has to agree, she *has* to." But what he'd do if she didn't, he didn't know. There was a stubborn look about Anne Sheridan, as sweet and innocent as she was, that worried him. Something about the set of her slender shoulders, the tilt of her chin that concerned him. If she'd really made up her mind, he didn't know how he'd change it. She seemed impervious to whatever charm he had.

During the meeting Rafik couldn't keep his eyes off the door to the outer office. But no one came in. No one knocked and said, "You have a call, Rafik, it's from a Ms. Sheridan." No matter how much he willed it to happen, it didn't. Instead his father gave him a steely look from time to time, no doubt to see if he was paying attention. When the meeting finally broke up and Rafik walked out, Massoud's secretary stopped him and handed him a slip of paper.

"I got a call?" he said to Ruth. "I thought I said…"

"Yes, I know," she said. "I told her to hold on and I'd get you, but she insisted on leaving a message."

"Yes, what was the message?" he asked, staring at the paper which only said "Anne called" and the time of her call.

"She said to tell you she can come to the gala after all."

"That's it? That's all she said?" Had she changed her mind about posing as his fiancée also?

"That's it. I'm sorry," Ruth said.

"*You're* sorry," he muttered as he walked down the hall to his office. If only he'd been able to speak to Anne, he could have judged her mood, found out why she'd changed her mind, and if she'd changed her mind about the fiancée part, too. Once in his office with the door closed, he dialed her number, but there was no answer. He left a message on her machine.

"Anne, I got your message and I'm very happy you can make it to the gala. I'll pick you up that night at your house. I'm sorry I didn't get a chance to talk to you. Give me a call at the office so we can firm up our plans. Did I say that I am very glad you can come?" Yes, of course he'd said that. He was repeating himself, and making a fool of himself, no doubt. He had so much to say to her, and it was frustrating not to be able to say it in person. He hung up and stared out the window for a long time before he could get back to work.

Chapter Four

It was a cool, damp morning on the marshes some thirty miles south of San Francisco along the San Mateo County coast. At least twenty bird-watchers were out holding binoculars to their eyes watching herons swoop into the reeds looking for food.

"Some people would think we were crazy to get up at six to watch birds," Anne remarked to her friend Sally. "But I wouldn't miss it for the world. Who knows, I might even add a new bird to my list today."

"That's the fun of it," Sally agreed. "You never know what you're going to see."

"And it's so peaceful, so quiet. The world is new and fresh." Anne sighed. "It makes me feel a lot better when I'm out here."

Sally put her binoculars down and gave Anne a sideways glance. "School's out. You're on vacation. Anything wrong?" she asked

"No, of course not," Anne said. "It's just...well I am a little worried. I'm going to a gala ball on Saturday night."

"How exciting. What's to be worried about?"

"Oh...uh..." How to explain that the problem was one overbearing sheik who'd caused her no end of troubles since she'd first met him at the wedding. Him and his search for a fiancée. Him and his teasing about what happened that night in the hotel. Then there was her headmistress's assumptions and Anne's need to protect her own reputation. She couldn't bring herself to mention any one of these things, so she brought up the one problem she could mention.

"I don't know what to wear to a gala."

"You don't have anything?"

"Nothing but a pink bridesmaid dress I wore to my friend's wedding. I'm sure that won't do, and besides, I really don't want to wear it again." She said this with a little more vehemence than absolutely necessary. The dress brought back memories of traipsing through the lobby of the hotel, standing in the middle of Montgomery Street looking up at the sheik's office building and entering his office without her shoes on. She had stuffed the dress to the back of her closet and didn't ever want to see it again.

"I'd be happy to go shopping with you," Sally offered. "If you're thinking of buying something new."

"That's exactly what I was thinking. Would you really?"

"Really. I'm even free this afternoon."

"I would love that. I can't tell you how much that means to me. First, I have no idea what's appropriate and second, I...I need support. I don't go to galas very often. In fact, I've never been to one."

"Neither have I," Sally said. "But I've seen the pictures in the society section of the newspaper of the charity balls, so I kind of know what the women wear. And I know the tickets cost upwards of a thousand dollars."

"A piece?" Anne was shocked. Though she shouldn't have been.

"I assume your date can afford it," Sally said.

"Yes, I...I assume he can."

"This is so exciting to have an excuse to buy a special dress. Lucky you."

"Lucky?" Anne murmured. "I'm not sure about that."

After a stop at home to change out of her knee-high boots and fleece jacket, Anne met her friend for lunch in the food court of the mall before they went to the fancy dress section of one of the large department stores. Sally wasn't the only one who thought it was exciting to be invited to a gala ball and have the chance to buy a new dress for it. The sales clerk also got into the spirit and threw herself into the task, bringing in dress after dress. Some were long and sequined. Some were short and strapless. Another was bright red and form-fitting.

"Stunning with her hair," the clerk declared, standing back for a long look.

"I feel too conspicuous," Anne said. "I never wear red."

"Hmm," Sally said. "With your skin I think something in black might work better."

The clerk nodded and went back out on the floor to look for more dresses.

"I assume your date will be in black tie," Sally said.

"My date? Oh, yes, my date," Anne said, taking a seat on the dressing room bench while she waited for the saleswoman. "Actually he's just a friend, no, more of an acquaintance. He only asked me because he's new in town and doesn't know many women. I really don't know what he's wearing. I haven't talked to him since he asked me. We've been playing phone tag."

This was a lie. Anne was letting her answering machine

take her messages so she wouldn't have to talk to Rafik. She had nothing to say to him on the phone. She knew she'd have to broach the subject of the pretend engagement sooner or later, but she preferred that it be later. As late as possible.

"Whatever he wears," Anne continued, "it will be appropriate, I know that for sure."

The dress they all agreed on, Sally, Anne and the clerk, was a floor-length black chiffon dress that was bare on one shoulder and had a wispy scarf that they showed her how to toss over the other shoulder. The fabric clung very snugly to her curves then flared out before it hit the floor. While Anne stood in front of the mirror, the other two women voiced their approval.

"Stunning."

"Sensational."

"Makes her skin look like porcelain."

"Elegant."

"Sexy in a subdued way."

Anne blushed. But she did like the dress. She felt like everything they said she looked. Even sexy. She also felt a tingle of excitement at the thought of the ball, almost overriding her dread at seeing Rafik again.

Next was the shoe salon where Sally kept the salesman busy bringing out pair after pair of strappy sandals until they found some that were under four inches high so she wouldn't throw her back out in the first half hour.

"As for a pedicure," Sally said, "I'd go with some gorgeous shade of Jungle Red."

A pedicure? She'd never had one in her life.

"I'll give you the name of my nail salon," Sally offered, as if she'd read Anne's thoughts.

"Thank you."

Before the two friends parted in the parking lot of the

mall, Sally told Anne she'd help her get ready that night, if she wanted her to. "I'm no good at nails, but I could blow-dry your hair if you don't want to sit in a beauty salon all day."

"I'd love some help. I'm going to be a nervous wreck," Anne confessed.

"I'll bring my makeup kit, too," Sally said. "Not that you need any. Just a hint of blush, maybe and some eye shadow."

Anne thought she'd hate subjecting herself to a pedicure, but she loved it. Especially the foot massage that came with it. It put her into a state of relaxed nirvana that lasted for hours. But as time passed that day, she gradually lost her composure. She was glad to see Sally arrive to distract her from her thoughts and worries and also because applying mascara when one's hand is shaking is a recipe for disaster. Sally, on the other hand, was cool and calm and collected and her hands were steady. Of course she wasn't going to a ball with a sheik who some people thought she was already engaged to.

"Tell me more about your date," Sally said as she zipped up Anne's dress.

"He's not really..."

"I know he's not really your date. But he is calling for you, isn't he? That sounds like a date to me."

"I think it's more like he's afraid I won't go to the ball if he doesn't come and get me," Anne explained. "As I said, he doesn't know many women in town and that's why I got invited."

"Well, I'll just slip away before he comes then so I won't be in the way," Sally said.

"No," Anne said. "Don't leave. I might do something rash. Like run away." She laughed nervously, but that's exactly what she wanted to do. Run as far as she could so she didn't have to face the man. Because she was going to have to swallow her pride and explain why she needed a fiancé as much as he did.

Sally laughed too at the ridiculousness of the idea of her running away in her new black dress from a gala ball. But then she didn't know the whole story. Anne was afraid that she herself didn't know the whole story either. And neither did Rafik for that matter. He didn't know about her headmistress and the pressure on her and though he'd told her his side of the story, she didn't know what really happened that night. She sighed and the doorbell rang. Her heart stopped beating for one moment, then she took a deep breath and went to the door.

Instantly all of the air in her lungs seemed to rush out, leaving her totally out of breath. He was that handsome. She'd seen him in a tuxedo before, but somehow she hadn't appreciated his dark good looks before. Maybe it was the porch light shining on his coal-black hair. Maybe it was the gasp she heard Sally make when she saw him. Maybe it was that he was simply the most attractive man she'd ever met. Physically, that is.

Anne stepped back, and Rafik walked through the open door. He too seemed to have lost his ability to speak. He just stood staring at her. Of course, she looked a little different from the last time he'd been there when she was in dungarees and a T-shirt.

Finally she caught her breath and remembered her manners. "I...Rafik this is my friend Sally. She came by to...uh..."

"To say hello," Sally said. "Happy to meet you, Rafik. I'll be off now. You two have a wonderful time."

At the door, Rafik engaged Sally in conversation before she left while Anne went to get her wool coat. She could tell by the look on Sally's face she thought he was charming. He didn't even know how charming he was being, she thought. It was so much a part of him. But Sally knew. Before she left, she gave Anne a knowing wink and a thumbs-up. Then they were on their own. In the car they talked about the weather and about the newlyweds who were back from their honeymoon. They talked about anything but the matters at hand. Anne was grateful that he was a good conversationalist.

She dreaded silence between them. Silence would give her time to think and worry. It would give her time to think about him and what she had to ask him. She was only too aware of the way he surrounded her with soft music from his sound system, the smell of leather and the heated seats. It was luxury pure and simple. Of course she'd been in this car before, but she hadn't been alert enough to appreciate the quiet purr of the engine and the skill of the driver. He kept up an effortless stream of conversation without any mention of an engagement, false or otherwise.

When they arrived at the historic hotel on Market Street, Rafik helped Anne from the car.

"May I be the first to say before we go inside, that you look very beautiful tonight?" he said in his deep quiet voice.

"Thank you," she said. She was afraid he said that to all his dates. Maybe flattery was just one of the tools he used to get what he wanted. But he sounded sincere. He looked sincere, too. His dark eyes were fixed on hers and of course she wanted to believe him. She also wanted to tell him how very gorgeous he looked, but she thought he probably already knew that and she was way too shy to say anything so personal anyway.

They walked into the high-ceilinged ballroom together, arm in arm. The scent of expensive perfume was in the air.

The candles in gold sconces along the wall gave off a warm light. The tight knot of nervousness in the pit of Anne's stomach relaxed somewhat. Rafik put his hand on the small of her back, a gesture which might have been annoying coming from someone else, but tonight in that atmosphere, it felt protective and reassuring.

Rafik introduced her to many people, whose names she instantly forgot. She met his mother, who was a small and graceful older woman with silver hair swept back from her unlined face. She told Anne how much she had been looking forward to meeting her.

"My sons and my husband have told me so much about you," Nura Harun said in lightly accented English. "Rafik," she chided her son. "You didn't tell me she was so beautiful."

He smiled. "I wanted to surprise you, Mother. In any case, Anne's looks are secondary to her good nature."

"I'm delighted to meet you at last," the older woman said. "I didn't have a chance at the wedding." Then she asked Anne how she knew Carolyn and posed some questions about her teaching job. Apparently satisfied by what she had learned, she shooed them toward the dance floor. "Now don't let me keep you from enjoying the party," she said.

Rafik led Anne to the dance floor. Out of the corner of his eye he saw his parents in earnest discussion while their glances followed him and Anne. He could just imagine what they were saying. How happy they must be, thinking what a good choice Anne would be for him. She would be too if he wanted to get married. But he didn't. At least not for quite some time. After he'd had his fill of playing the field. When he'd learned how to judge women better.

As for Anne, he didn't know if she was interested in marriage, but if she was, he was quite certain it wouldn't be to him. She'd made it clear he was not her type. But that didn't mean she couldn't do him a small favor and pretend to be his fiancée.

He was just going to ask her about that little favor, but once he put his arms around her, and her hair brushed his cheek and the fragrance of her skin filled his senses, he couldn't do it. He didn't want to spoil the mood. She fitted perfectly in his arms, as if she'd been made for him. Which was probably what his parents were thinking as they watched them dance.

He probably ought to move away, just put a little distance between them to avoid any gossip, if possible. But she felt so good, so right in his arms. He pressed her close and heard her sigh softly. He didn't know what it meant. But if she'd wanted to pull away, she could have. After a few songs, he thought of taking a break and getting a glass of champagne for each of them, but he didn't want to break the spell. The music, the soft lights and a beautiful woman in his arms. What more could a man want?

She didn't speak and neither did he. What was there to say? He wished the music would never end. When it did end, and the orchestra took a break, they stayed where they were, hand in hand, their gazes locked on each other. What did he see in her eyes? He saw something he'd never seen before. Something he hadn't seen in any other women he'd romanced. And there had been quite a few. They were usually beautiful, always sexy and self-assured. They played the same games he did. They knew the rules. Nobody gets involved and nobody gets hurt. They were fun and exciting. You could talk to these women, laugh with them and love them. For a while.

Anne was not one of these women. She was different. In her eyes he saw honesty and trust. He saw a woman without pretense, without guile. A woman who didn't know the rules. And that scared him. It scared him so much he wanted to run away. But even more he wanted to stay. Stay with her in his arms there on the dance floor forever.

He thought he knew a lot about women. But he didn't know how to handle Anne. The music started again, and she went into his arms without a word, as if it was meant to be. So much for his running away. He knew there were other couples around, he knew that the lights went up again and then dimmed, he knew that time was passing, but all he really knew was that he wanted the night to go on forever.

He wondered if Anne felt the same. He couldn't get over how stunning she looked tonight. Her one bare shoulder tantalized him. He wanted to bare the other one, too. He wanted to press his lips against her skin. He wanted to inhale her scent and never let her go. She was by far the most beautiful woman in the room. The sexiest and the most desirable. And she was his. His for tonight, anyway.

She was his until his brother tapped him on the shoulder and cut in. Before he could tell him to buzz off and leave them alone, Rahman introduced himself to Anne.

"Hello," Rahman said to Anne. "I don't believe we've met, but I've heard so much about you. I'm Rahman, the younger, good-looking twin. I'm sure you don't mind leaving my brother for a dance or two. You two have been at it forever as my parents have noted. It's time you stopped monopolizing this lovely lady, Rafik," he said to his brother.

"Get lost," Rafik said, glaring at his brother. "Go find somebody else to dance with. Anne is taken."

"Really? That sounds serious. By the way, Rafik, the parents want a word with you. They're getting ideas."

"Ideas. What does that mean? Oh, all right." Rafik recognized the determined look on his brother's face and he didn't want to make a scene on the dance floor, so he clamped his lips together and walked away just as he heard his brother saying to Anne, "May I say that you look sensational tonight?"

Rafik almost turned around and cut back in, but he didn't want to overreact. His brother was a born flirt. He used words like that all the time. Most women didn't take him seriously. But Anne was different. She might think he was serious. He looked serious, Rafik thought with a quick glance over his shoulder. It was a mistake to look backward, he realized, as he ran right into his parents. He found that they were positively beaming at him.

His father put his arm around his shoulder. "We're very pleased with your choice of partner, Rafik," Massoud said. "She's a lovely girl."

"Partner? You mean dance partner, of course. Yes she is very lovely, Father, but don't get the wrong idea."

"I couldn't possibly get the wrong idea about such a woman," Massoud said. "Nor could your mother. We all agree you couldn't have made a better choice."

Choice? Choice of partner? Did his father mean choice of dance partner or life partner? He was just about to warn his father not to jump to conclusions, but at that moment a business acquaintance interrupted them with some news of an investment prospect for his father. Rafik leaned against the wall by himself moodily watching his brother dance with his date. Not only dance, but talk animatedly, as if they were old friends. Anne didn't seem shy at all. He regarded them with narrowed eyes, hoping Rahman would feel his animosity from there and give her back to him. How soon would it be proper to cut in on them, he wondered. And why didn't his brother find his own woman to dance with?

He couldn't stand it another moment. He went out to the

dance floor and as politely as possible told his brother it was his turn now. Rahman shrugged and retreated.

"I'm sorry you got stuck with my brother," Rafik said, taking Anne into his arms again.

"I wasn't stuck," she said. "I enjoyed talking to him."

"More than you enjoy talking to me?" he asked.

She blushed but didn't answer. Maybe because the answer was yes.

"You've made quite an impression on my family," Rafik said.

"They seem very nice, but I hardly know them," she protested.

"They like what they see," he said. "I'm afraid that's your fault. You look beautiful and you're charming, too. I'm afraid they're going to be disappointed when they find out you're not going to be my fiancée. That is if you haven't reconsidered my proposition."

Anne knew what she had to say. She just couldn't say it. Now that she needed him to pretend as much as he needed her, she was tongue-tied. When she was in his arms, swaying to the music, her head against his chest, she felt as if she was made of molten lava. The way he looked at her made her feel very desirable. His arms around her made her feel soft and fragile and protected.

But then that was his way. He was born to seduce women. Pretending anything with him could be very dangerous. Like playing with fire. She reminded herself that he was a handsome, rich man who only wanted a fiancée to please his parents. As he'd told her, he had no intention of getting engaged or married for real. But she was not a player the way he was. She was a vulnerable young woman who'd never had a serious boyfriend. Any more romancing, dancing and flattery and she might succumb and start believing...that fantasy was reality. She'd allowed herself to come under the spell of the night and the music and the man. Now was the time to shake off these romantic delusions and face the facts.

She knew what she had to do. She must tell him now that she couldn't possibly reconsider any scheme to fool his parents. Not for her sake or theirs. Yes, it might cause her a problem at the school, but she'd have to deal with that. It would be better than tricking his family, whom she was beginning to like. His brother was amusing and fun and his parents seemed very kind and not at all overbearing. If he was going to disappoint them, that was his problem. They had no business fooling such nice people as that.

The music stopped and she pulled away out of Rafik's arms and immediately felt the loss. She realized she could spend hours in his arms, with his breath fanning her cheek, the scent of his skin and his clothes surrounding her, seducing her. Making her want more. Yes, it was time to put an end to this charade. He was not interested in her except as a novelty, and she was not interested in him. She didn't belong in this society any more than a robin belongs in an aviary. She dropped one hand from his shoulder but he didn't let go of the other.

"Rafik," she said. "I have no intention..."

A hush fell over the room as his father stepped onto the bandstand. The drummer executed a drumroll. Anne had a feeling of foreboding. She wished she'd spoken to Rafik earlier.

"What does this mean?" she whispered.

"I don't know," he said, his forehead drawn in a frown.

"Ladies and gentlemen," Sheik Massoud Harun began. "We have invited you here tonight to get to know you. And for you to get to know us. We are strangers here in San Francisco, but you have made us feel welcome. My

wife and I have the honor to announce the engagement of
our elder son, Rafik.''

Anne felt the blood drain from her face. "What on
earth..." she murmured.

"What did you tell him?"

"I told him not to get the wrong idea," he muttered.
"But apparently he did. He told me he was pleased with
my choice of a partner. I thought he meant dance partner.
I should have known. Don't worry. It's just a misunderstanding. I'll straighten him out."

"He seems to be beckoning to us," Anne said. She felt
her face flame. She wished she could find a hole and hide.
Instead she felt all eyes on her as she and Rafik walked
hand in hand to the bandstand. How would he tell his father
that it was a mistake when everyone in the whole room was
clapping, the orchestra was playing something romantic and
the lights had been turned up so everyone could see them?

In fact, telling his father at this moment would be next
to impossible. She knew and Rafik must also know that his
family would be humiliated. So they stood next to his parents on the bandstand for what seemed to be an eternity.
She smiled until she felt her face would crack while Rafik
whispered in her ear that she was not to worry, that he'd
fix everything.

When they'd received congratulations from dozens,
maybe hundreds of strangers, they finally filed into the dining room where white tables were set up for a sumptuous
buffet. Seeing the pride on Rafik's parents' faces, she knew
he couldn't tell them now. With her plate full of lobster
thermidor and slices of rare roast beef, tiny new potatoes
and green beans amandine, she was seated between Rafik
and his mother. Rafik seemed subdued. She couldn't blame
him. He had an enormous task ahead of him, telling his
parents it was all a mistake. Anne supposed she too ought

to be subdued, knowing she had an unpleasant task ahead of her, trying to explain to her headmistress that she was no longer engaged.

Fortunately there was no more dancing after the dinner. Rafik promised they'd leave as soon as possible, but so many people wanted to talk to him and congratulate him, it took at least another hour to get away. It was an hour of agony for Anne. She could hardly bear to look at his parents and listen to them telling everyone how happy they were for the young couple. She could tell that both his mother and father were genuinely pleased. That this was something they had wanted for a long time. She seriously wondered how Rafik would be able to burst their bubble and tell them it wasn't true.

Rafik's mother took her aside and told her how happy she was. "We will have to get to know each other better," Nura said.

Anne didn't know what to say. All she could manage was a nervous smile.

"We don't have a house yet for entertaining, but I would like to invite you to tea at the hotel. They tell me they do it rather nicely. Nothing like the Dorchester in London, of course, but if you are free one day...?"

Again, Anne could only smile, which seemed enough encouragement for Rafik's mother.

"Shall we say Tuesday then? Since you are a schoolteacher—such a suitable occupation for a young unmarried woman—then I hope you will be free to join me. Meet me in the lobby of the St. Francis at two, if that is convenient."

Anne nodded. How could she say no? How could she say anything at all with her throat clogged? Nura was so kind and would be so disappointed when she learned the truth. Anne hoped she wouldn't have to face her after that happened. As soon as Rafik explained that the engagement was not for real, the invitation would probably be recalled.

In the car on the way back to her house Rafik promised her that he would tell them.

"Just do me a favor and give me a little time," he said as he pulled up in front of her house.

If this wasn't the time for Anne to ask Rafik a favor, then the time was never, she thought. "Actually," she said. "I have a favor to ask of you, too."

"Anything," he said, turning to face her from the driver's seat. In the light from the streetlight, she could see his dark eyes glowing and his jaw jutting forward. His features were strong, just like his personality. She had the feeling she could ask him anything and he'd do it for her. She thought that if he gave his word he wouldn't let her down.

"I'm in a bit of trouble at my school," she began.

"No," he said, anxiously. "What is it? What can I do to help?"

"It seems that some of the parents saw me that night at the hotel when I was…uh…when you were carrying me up to your room. I don't know how it happened, but they got the wrong idea."

A small smile briefly played on the sheik's lips, then he was serious. "I'm sorry about that," he said. "I would have done anything possible to spare you the embarrassment, but I was caught in a situation that wasn't entirely of my own making." He didn't say whose making it was, but they both understood that she had to take part of the blame for her condition.

"I understand," she said, "but they didn't understand. Though the headmistress can't dictate what the teachers do in their free time, naturally she and the board of directors want us all to be above suspicion."

"Of course. So what can I do? Speak to your headmistress and to the board? Explain…"

"Explain what? That I wasn't really inebriated? After all, I did have two glasses of champagne. Or that I really didn't spend the night with you in your bed? You can't deny that, can you?" Anne squeezed her hands into tight fists, realizing that now was the time to ask him what really happened that night. "You say that nothing happened between us. And I believe you. I just want to know why. Was I so unattractive? Was I that unappealing? You're a sheik. A playboy by your own admission. A man who doesn't want to get engaged or married. A man who's looking for women to seduce. Can you tell me what made you leave me and my virtue untouched?" she blurted. By the time she'd finished saying the things that had bothered her since that night, her voice had risen and tears had sprung to her eyes.

"Anne," he said, taking her hands in his and stroking her ice-cold fingers until they were warm and supple. "Believe me, you were very appealing. So appealing, so seductive and so attractive that it took all my willpower to leave you on your side of the bed. To undress you and not touch your body. I know what you must think of me. You're right, people say I'm a playboy, and I've earned that reputation. But even playboys have scruples. Sheiks have rules. One of them is that the woman must be awake and willing. I have never forced myself on a woman. I've never needed to and I never will."

Anne let go of a breath she was holding. Her whole body was flooded with relief.

"If the day or night comes along when you are willing, then I would make love to you most tenderly, most exquisitely. I would take your clothes off, not the way I did that night but…"

Anne felt her face burning and her limbs trembling at the thought of being seduced by the sheik. "Please," she said.

"Please what?" he said lightly. "You'll have to be more specific. Please stop, Rafik, or please start?"

"Stop," she gasped. "I'm not used to men like you. I don't have affairs with sheiks, or anybody for that matter."

"You mean you've never...?"

"Never. I'm a...virgin." It was hard to say the word, but necessary. He needed to know who she was and what she was before they went any further in this strange relationship.

There was a long silence. Anne couldn't look him in the eye. She didn't want to see his shock and surprise at finding himself in the company of a twenty-eight-year-old virgin.

"I see," he said gravely. "And this is because of moral scruples or...?"

"It's for all sorts of reasons," she said. "I don't believe in indiscriminate sex and it's also for lack of opportunity."

"I don't believe that," he said.

She told him then about the disease she'd suffered in high school when she had to wear a brace. She told him how unattractive she'd felt. How she'd missed out on a normal adolescence. He listened gravely, and when she'd finished he told her how touched he was that she'd confided in him.

"I will treasure your confidence," he said, tracing his finger around the curve of her cheek. "And endeavor to deserve your trust in me. Now what was the favor you were going to ask me?"

The mere touch of his finger made it almost impossible to think. But with an effort, Anne remembered what it was she needed to ask him. "Oh, yes, it was about my school and the headmistress. In an effort to explain my behavior I told her that you were my fiancé.''

Rafik smiled.

''I know what you're thinking. That I'm impulsive and dishonest. I can't explain what came over me. What I said didn't make sense, but she'd caught me off guard. I wanted her to know that I was not in the company of a stranger, someone I'd just met at a wedding, for example. So I said the first thing that came into my head. After all that talk about a fiancée, the word just popped out. Yes, I know I was borrowing a page from your book. For some reason I thought it might explain why I was in the hotel that night with you in a very compromising situation.''

''Did it work?'' he asked.

''I guess it did, because the next thing I knew the head-mistress had forgotten how disturbed she was and she was arranging an engagement party for you to meet the staff. It's a kind of tradition, an effort to instill the feeling that our staff is one big happy family.''

''So I'm to be a part of your family just as you are of mine,'' he said.

''Only temporarily,'' she assured him.

''Of course,'' he said. ''I'd be delighted.''

''Would you really? I'm afraid it might be awkward for you.''

''I think I can handle it.''

''Yes, I suppose you can,'' she said. Why did she doubt that Rafik would be completely at ease in any social situation and charm every single faculty member without any effort?

''Then it's settled,'' he said. ''We have an agreement. I suggest we seal it with a kiss.''

Once again she was caught off guard. Not that she hadn't thought about his kissing her. While they were dancing with his body pressed against hers, it was hard not to think about kissing him. She'd imagined it happening more than once. But when it happened it was not the kind of kiss she expected. It was not the kind of kiss between two parties merely sealing an agreement. It was the kind of kiss that an engaged couple would exchange if they were madly in love. It was the kind of kiss that lovers who have been holding back for one reason or another would exchange. It was full of passion and pent-up frustration finally let loose.

Not at first. The first kiss was a mere whisper of his lips against hers. A promise of things to come. Then he pulled back for a moment and framed her face with his hands. He looked deep into her eyes as if searching for something, a sign or a wish, and then, when he appeared to be satisfied with what he saw, his lips met hers once again. This time for real.

She wrapped her arms around his neck and angled her mouth to meet his. She had never been kissed like this. So deeply, so profoundly and so passionately. She'd never kissed anyone like that either, with all her heart and soul. Somewhere deep inside her she knew she shouldn't. She knew it was all pretend, and it would come back to haunt her some day. But she couldn't stop herself. And she certainly didn't want to stop him.

His kisses made her feel like she was on a fast train. It was a thrilling ride and where it would end she didn't know or care. The ride was all that mattered. She slid into his arms from across the leather seat of his car. His lips moved to the hollow of her throat, then to her bare shoulder. She shivered.

"Are you cold?" he murmured.

"No, I'm on fire," she murmured. She really felt like she might burn up. She was radiating heat, she knew her skin must be hot to the touch, every nerve ending was tingling, and she thought she might burst into flames if anyone held a match up to her.

She felt his lips curve in a smile against her bare skin. She tangled her fingers in his dark hair. He smelled so good. Like leather and exotic spice and fine soap. She could hear his heart pounding in time to her own. How had this happened? She, an innocent schoolteacher, was locked in the arms of a rich and experienced man she barely knew. Or did she know him better than she thought?

Then she stopped thinking and gave in to the sensations that spiraled through her. Rafik pulled her across his legs until she was in his lap. He cradled her in his arms and, as tight as it was in his front seat, she settled there as if she could stay forever. He was kissing her lips again, teasing her by slowly nibbling at them, and then his mouth was open and he was using his tongue to turn up the heat even further. Shyly she opened her mouth to him and met his tongue with hers. It was incredible. She'd never felt such intimacy with anyone. She never dreamed that something so daring could feel so right.

"I can feel your heart pounding, Anne," he said breathlessly. "I don't want to stop, but I must. I'm afraid I'm going to have to take you in now." She pulled back and looked down, afraid to meet his gaze. Once again he'd called a halt to what might have been. She was confused. Wasn't the woman supposed to be the one to say no? What was wrong with her? Did she really have no morals? Didn't she know when to say no? Was her abstinence only because of lack of opportunity as she'd said? Her face was hot with shame. She untangled herself from him and reached for the door handle. Before he could come around and open it for her, she was out of the car and on the sidewalk.

"Wait a minute," he said catching her by the hand.

"I can see myself in," she said, pulling away. "Thank you very much."

"I've offended you," he said. "What have I said to hurt you?"

"Nothing. Nothing at all. Good night."

He stood on the sidewalk and watched her unlock her front door. She could feel his bafflement at her behavior, but she couldn't stop herself. She couldn't explain herself either. It was too humiliating. She stood inside the darkened living room, leaning against the closed front door and listened for the sound of his car engine. When she finally heard it she sagged against the door. Her lips were swollen, her face was flushed and her whole body ached as though she'd been pounded with a mallet. All she could think was that it was a good thing they weren't really engaged. She was relieved knowing that he wasn't really her fiancé. If pretending had left her in this state of semi-consciousness, what would a real engagement do to her? She shuddered at the thought.

Chapter Five

The handball courts at the Pacific Heights Health Club were crowded. By the time the brothers started playing, it was almost six o'clock in the evening. Rafik was full of nervous energy. He'd had a terrible day during which he had accepted numerous congratulations on his engagement, tried to get in touch with Anne to no avail, attended some tedious meetings, and put up with his brother's remarks. He was looking forward to beating Rahman at handball and perhaps shutting him up for a while.

After a half hour they were both tired and sweat poured off their faces. They'd each won a set and neither wanted to give up without being the victor.

"You used to beat me," Rahman said. "Your mind wasn't on the game tonight."

"If you know so much, what was it on then?" Rafik asked, wiping his face on a towel in the locker room.

"Your fiancée perhaps? I still don't know how you pulled it off."

"I didn't pull it off. Father made the announcement and

I still don't know what got into him. I never said Anne had agreed to the engagement.''

"Don't blame Father. He saw what everyone else saw. You two were oblivious to the world for hours out there on the dance floor. He assumed you were serious about each other. So did I.''

"Wait a minute. Did you have anything to do with this?''

"Who, me?''

Rafik shot a glance at his brother. His innocent expression didn't fool him for a minute. "What did you do? What did you say?'' he demanded.

"I really don't remember. In any case you got what you wanted. You can't deny you needed a fiancée. Now you've got one. I can see I'll get no thanks for helping you out. Besides I didn't notice Ms. Anne Sheridan protesting.''

"What did you expect, that she'd stand up there in front of all those people and say it was all a mistake? She's too polite for that. She went along with it. But I can't say she's happy about it. Neither am I.''

"Of course you are. It's what you wanted. A stand-in fiancée which pleases the parents and gets you off the hook. Remember it's just for a short time. From the looks of you two on the dance floor I can't believe it's much of a hardship on either of you.''

"You don't think so? I don't know. I can't figure her out. Anne is the strangest girl. First she's cool then she's hot. She comes to the gala but she won't answer my calls.''

"Maybe she's busy. Maybe she's not sitting at the phone waiting for you to call her. That would be a blow to your ego, wouldn't it?''

"No, it wouldn't. I don't want a woman who has nothing to do but wait for me to call. She's got a life and I like that about her.''

"What else do you like about her? Her red hair? Her gorgeous body?"

Rafik snapped a towel at his brother. "Enough. She's a nice girl. But she's not my type. She's way too serious." But even as he said the words, he conjured up her face, he remembered how she felt in his arms and how she responded to his kisses. She *was* too serious for him or was he too much of a lightweight for her?

"Have you bought her a ring yet? I'm only asking because Father asked me."

"A ring? No, do I have to do that? I suppose I do. Aren't you supposed to take your fiancée with you to pick it out?"

"How should I know? I've never been engaged. I'll let you lead the way as always. What happens to the ring when you break your engagement?"

Rafik shrugged. "I'll let her have it. I'll owe her for being such a sport about it."

"Then go for it," his brother said.

Before Rafik could change his mind, he punched in her phone number on his cell phone. Maybe this time he'd get lucky and actually get to talk to her.

"Anne? Thank God I got you. We have to talk."

She sounded so subdued. And she declined his offer to come by her house. She finally agreed to meet him at a bar near the health club. "But only for a short time," she said.

"Why is that?" he asked. "You don't have another date, do you? Remember you're engaged to me."

"Not really."

"No, but…maybe we need to talk about that." He couldn't have her dating other men when it was imperative she appear to be engaged to him. Of course, the same applied to him, but he realized that he had no desire to date anyone else. He didn't know many other women in town anyway, but one seemed to be all he could handle at this time.

"Wouldn't it be easier if I dropped by your house?" he said.

"No." Anne didn't want him invading her privacy. His last visit to her garden had left an indelible impression. Every time she went out there she pictured him sitting on her bench. Every time she smelled the lavender, she remembered him crushing it between his fingers. "I'll meet you at the bar you mentioned."

He told her the address on Laguna. She said she'd be there in an hour. How could she say no again? But she was not accustomed to meeting men in bars on weeknights, or any nights for that matter.

So she went. Feeling totally out of her element, she sidled her way through the crowd of yuppies, hearing snatches of their conversations.

"Didn't I see you at Tahoe last weekend?"

"You remind me of someone I know."

"I heard you quit your job. How's it going?"

"I got laid off."

"That's nothing. My stock options just evaporated."

"Did you hear about Brian? He just got made partner."

She felt totally out of place in this world. Was this the kind of place and the kind of people Rafik frequented? If it was, it was a good thing this was a fake engagement, because if this was his scene, then they were even more different than she'd thought. Where was he? If he didn't show up in two more minutes she was going home. It had taken her a half hour to find a place to park in the neighborhood. Now she couldn't find him. Her nerves were frazzled. What did he want to talk about, anyway, that couldn't be discussed on the phone?

Just when she was about to give up, she saw him in the

corner at a table by himself, a glass of beer in front of him and a frown on his face. When he saw her, the frown faded. He got to his feet and beckoned her to the table.

"I was worried that you'd never come," he said.

"I had a hard time finding a parking place," she said, taking a seat opposite him. He was wearing a leather jacket and he looked like many of the other men in the place except more attractive than any one of them. It was the bronzed color of his skin and his coal-black hair and eyes. She didn't know if she'd ever get used to the way he looked at her. Even now. Even before they'd had their discussion, whatever it was. He looked at her with so much intensity she felt trapped by the look in his eyes. Did he do that to everyone? Was it all part of his allure that he turned off or on to women?

She studied his face. He didn't look unhappy. He just looked a little anxious with his eyebrows knitted together. She hoped he'd forgotten how she'd stormed out of the car after the ball the other night. She realized now how immature she must have seemed. Even worse, it might have seemed that she was upset because he hadn't seduced her the night of the wedding. Now *there* was a ridiculous thought.

"This was your idea to meet here," he said. "I would have been happy to come to your house. Now what would you like to drink? Some champagne?"

She stiffened. "Please don't remind me. I'll have coffee. What do you want to talk about?"

He hesitated while he ran his hand around his beer glass. "I can't tell my parents the engagement isn't for real," he said.

"But you said..."

"I know I did and I tried, but they're so happy about it, so pleased that I found someone like you...I just couldn't do it. All I can say is I'll have to wait a little while until things have cooled down a little. You have your reception at your school this week anyway, don't you?''

''Yes, if you're still willing to do it. I guess it won't hurt to continue a little longer.''

''Of course I'm willing. After what you put up with at the ball, it's the least I can do.''

''I promise you it won't last as long as the ball did.''

The corners of his mouth turned down. ''I had a good time. I thought you did, too. I hope you weren't bored,'' he said stiffly.

She blushed. ''No, that's not what I meant. I just wanted to assure you it would be a simple affair. It will be held in the old mansion of the school with just a few of the teachers there. Nothing special. But you will have to play the role of fiancé. By the way, your mother invited me to tea at the hotel next week.''

''I know. She told me. She always wanted a daughter. I think she thinks she's got one.''

''Oh, dear. I don't want to hurt her or your father. What should I do?''

''Go. Go have tea with her. It will make her happy.''

''And when she finds out…?''

He shook his head. ''They asked for it. They asked me for a fiancée and I've given them one. Who can say that any engagement will last? Of course we all hope for a happy ending. In their case a happy ending means my marriage. In my case…''

''Yes?'' she asked. She knew only too well that marriage was not his idea of a happy ending. She wanted to hear him say it, because it was something she had to engrave in her memory in case she started getting fooled into thinking this was all for real. Naturally, marrying a sheik was about as far from reality as she could get. She knew that.

"In my case, marriage is not one of my goals. Maybe one day when I'm older I will do my duty and marry, but not now."

"Of course. I understand."

"What about you, Anne, what would your parents say?"

"If they thought I was engaged? They'd be happy, I'm sure. But they live in Arizona and they're not likely to hear about it, not from me, anyway. So there will be no tears when it's over."

She imagined her mother hearing she was engaged to a sheik.

A sheik? You mean one of those Arab sheiks who come riding across the desert and carry you off to their tent, or is it their castle? Does he have a harem and oil wells?

"Who has the red hair in your family, is it your mother?" He reached across the table and twisted an auburn curl around his finger. She licked her lips. Why did he do these things? Why had he kissed her in the car? Why did he look at her that way? There was no one in the bar to impress or to fool into thinking they were really engaged. Then why...why...why...did he lean forward across the table and drink her in as if he was a thirsty man in the desert?

"My hair?" She was having a hard time coming up with an answer. It wasn't the question, it was him. He rattled her, he disturbed her and he knew it. "No, uh, it's my grandmother who had red hair. They say I look like her."

"She must have been beautiful," he said softly.

"I guess that's a compliment," she said.

"If I were to guess, I'd say you haven't had many."

"No. When I was small, the kids teased me and called me carrot-top. Then in high school...but I told you about high school. When I had scoliosis, I withdrew from social activities. No one noticed me or my hair. It was kind of a relief.''

"I can't believe no one noticed you," he said. "They must have been blind."

"Rafik, you don't need to compliment me," she said. "I've already agreed to this arrangement. It suits me as well as it suits you. I take responsibility for my part in the debacle at the wedding. I'm grateful to you for respecting my virtue that night and…and…so…" She didn't know how to make it any clearer.

"I don't understand," he said, leisurely unwrapping her hair from around his finger and leaning back against the bench. "Do you think what I say to you is calculated to win you over? It's not. I know what you think. That sheiks are all playboys. But we're not all bad. Give me credit for some sincerity."

"Of course. I didn't mean…" Now she was really confused. She'd hurt his feelings without meaning to.

"Surely someone before me has told you how beautiful you are."

She wanted to say yes. She wanted to brush off his compliments with a laugh or a shrug of her shoulders the way other women did, but she couldn't. The truth was that she'd never thought of herself as beautiful. She didn't know if anyone else did either, except some of her young students, none of whom was over six years old. Apparently her silence spoke volumes.

Rafik nodded. "I see," he said. She was afraid he did see. He saw too much.

"I must be going," she said, getting to her feet.

He put some money on the table and followed her out of the bar, with his hand resting possessively on her shoulder. She held her head high. She had to admit he made her feel attractive, appreciated and yes…even beautiful. Was that because he was skilled in the arts of flattery and pleasing women? Probably. Or was it, as he claimed, sincerity? How much she wanted to believe it was the latter.

He walked her to her car and paused. "Thank you for coming out tonight," he said. "You've made an awkward situation much better for me. I can't tell you how much I appreciate it."

She nodded, told him the time and place of the reception at her school. He told him he'd pick her up, and then he kissed her on the cheek before he opened her door for her.

She told herself there was no reason for her cheeks to burn up on the drive home. It was only a kiss on the cheek. But she was so inexperienced, she had so little defenses against the charm of a sheik. How was she to know what to do, what to say? She didn't know.

A few days later Carolyn, her newlywed friend, called her. Before Anne could ask about her honeymoon, Carolyn demanded to know if the rumor she had heard about Anne and Rafik was true.

"Sort of, I mean what did you hear exactly?" Anne asked cautiously. This was awful. She couldn't lie to her good friend. And yet if she told her the truth....

"Tarik said he heard you were engaged to his cousin. I told him it couldn't possibly be true. You just met him at the wedding, right?"

"Yes, of course, but it's not what you think," Anne said.

"Good, because he's not your type," Carolyn said.

"I know that, I definitely know that," Anne said.

"So how did the family get this crazy idea?" Carolyn asked.

"I can explain...I think. You see...Carolyn this is strictly between you and me. You can't breathe a word of this to anyone, especially anyone in the family."

"Even Tarik? I don't know if I can keep a secret from him."

"But can you trust him?"

"With my life," Carolyn said.

Anne sighed. How wonderful to be in love with someone you could trust that way. She took a deep breath. "All right, then. Here's what happened. Rafik needed a fiancée…"

"What for? He distinctly told me he wasn't interested in getting married."

"Yes, yes, exactly. That's why he needs a fiancée, not a real fiancée but just someone to act like one. That's what I'm doing."

"But why? Why would you do such a thing?"

"I…I don't know exactly except that he's a very persuasive person and the whole thing happened at the gala ball which you missed. It was a giant misunderstanding between him and his parents. They're set on his getting married, but, as you know, he has no intention of getting engaged or married. So for some reason when they saw us together at the ball, they assumed I was his fiancée and announced it to everybody."

"Oh, no."

"Oh, yes. I didn't know what to do. I couldn't get up there and say it wasn't true. Not when everyone was so happy, congratulating him and me. I was in a state of shock."

"And Rafik, what state was he in?" Carolyn asked.

"He was shocked, too. He says he'll explain it to them. Just not right now. Because he actually wants a fiancée, not a real one of course. A false one, someone who will pretend to be a fiancée, to get them off his case, so to speak."

"So everybody got what they wanted. Or at least they think they did. His parents got a future daughter-in-law whom they approve of, I would suppose. Who wouldn't approve of you?''

"As a matter of fact, they do. His mother invited me to tea and they both have been truly nice to me.''

"So the parents get you, Rafik gets off the hook, but what about you, what do you get out of it? I won't stand for Rafik taking advantage of you.''

"No, no, he isn't. He's been very good about the whole thing. And he's doing me a favor, too...." Anne stopped. She didn't want to go into the false engagement she'd gotten herself into with her headmistress, so she didn't finish her sentence, hoping Carolyn wouldn't notice.

"I hope he's doing you lots of favors," Carolyn said. "Because I don't see what you're getting out of it. What do you want out of it?''

Anne didn't know what to say. She didn't want to say *I want what you have. A husband who loves you and whom you can trust.* She didn't want to sound envious.

"Never mind," Carolyn said. "You don't have to tell me. I know you too well. You only want what's best for everyone else. But what's going to happen when everyone finds out?''

"That's what I'm worried about. But Rafik doesn't seem to be worried. He thinks he can just explain that the engagement was broken off. After all, it happens. It's happened to him once already, I understand. But I don't like it. I really don't. Especially if I have to get to know his parents. I feel like such a fraud.''

"That's got to be tough," Carolyn said sympathetically. "Oh, my. I'm overwhelmed. But believe me I won't tell anybody but Tarik, and I'll swear him to secrecy. But please, Anne, don't let yourself be taken advantage of. Because I won't sit by and let that happen. I know, Rafik is now a part of my family, but you are my friend and I'm responsible for introducing you to him.''

"I won't, believe me. I can take care of myself," she assured her friend. After she'd hung up, she paced around her living room, getting more worried by the minute. Wondering if she should have told Carolyn. But it felt so good to confide in someone. And the secret had begun to burn a hole in her psyche. On the other hand, the more people that knew about this charade, the more dangerous it became that the wrong people would find out. She sat down at her desk and looked at her calendar, checking off the obstacles ahead of her. First was tea with his mother. Then the reception at the school which she'd confirmed with the headmistress who had promised to gather together all the teachers and staff who were around during the summer.

After that she could relax and attend a seminar on new methods in teaching reading put on by the state teachers' association. It was to be held at a rustic lodge on the ocean near Monterey, and there would be no sheiks in attendance, just teaching colleagues from around the state. There would be stimulating, late-night sessions around the fireplace where they would exchange techniques for teaching children from the brightest to the most disadvantaged. There she could relax and be herself, a competent first-grade teacher who enjoyed her work and her life the way it was. No need to pretend anything in front of her fellow teachers. They knew who she was, and best of all, she knew who she was.

Rafik was trying to avoid his parents, afraid of having to enter into an awkward conversation about his "love life," but since he worked with Massoud in the office, it was difficult not to see him. The good thing was that they had plenty of business affairs to discuss, so avoiding the topic of Anne and his engagement hadn't been as hard to do as he'd imagined. It was his mother who caught him off guard one day in his office.

He jumped to his feet and kissed her on the cheek. "What a surprise," he said. "I thought you were busy furnishing your new apartment."

"I always have time for my sons," Nura said.

"I'll get Rahman," Rafik offered, reaching for his phone. "So we can all get together for a few minutes. Then I'm afraid I have to take off to see one of our clients." Rahman would be a good distraction. His mother couldn't possibly bear down on him with him in the room, too.

His mother shook her head. "I've just seen your brother. I know you're busy so I won't take a moment."

"Sit down," he said politely. He didn't like the determined look on her face. If it had anything to do with his future it could mean trouble.

She took a seat across from his desk and gave him a look that made him uneasy.

"I'm having tea with Anne today," she said.

"Ah, yes, she mentioned it to me. I'm sure she's looking forward to it."

"As am I," she said. "I just want to know if there is anything I shouldn't mention, such as your former fiancée."

"I would appreciate your discretion, Mother. There's no need to bring that up. It's past history."

"What about the time you fell off your polo pony and lost the match for your team?" she asked.

"Perhaps you should let me tell that story. We haven't known each other long enough to delve into each other's childhoods yet." But he realized that though they hadn't known each other very long at all, he already knew about Anne's scoliosis and the humiliation she had felt wearing a brace. It had helped him understand her shyness, and her unawareness of her charm and looks.

"Another thing, about the engagement...."

Rafik braced himself for the worst. And it came.

"I wondered if you'd set a wedding date yet?"

"Uh...no. Not yet. We both believe in long engagements. Especially considering what happened the last time."

"I hope your unhappy memories from the past won't prevent you from seeing the difference between Anne and your previous fiancée. They are as different as night and day, from what I can see."

"You couldn't be more right about that. Still we're in no hurry."

"You're over thirty," she reminded him.

"What about Rahman?" he asked. "He's over thirty, too."

She smiled. "I've spoken to Rahman."

"That's good. He needs to be spoken to."

Nura opened her mouth to say something else, but fortunately the telephone rang and when he hung up, his mother had left. He breathed a huge sigh of relief.

After his mother left, Rafik picked up the phone and called Anne's number but no one answered. He wanted to warn her to tell the same story to his mother, that she also believed in long engagements. He thought he could count on her. She most certainly wouldn't agree to a date no matter what his mother said to her. All the same, he would have liked to speak to her before she walked into tea with his mother. For a shy person like Anne, it could be likened to walking into a lion's den.

He knew that his mother, who seemed to be as traditional as a wife could be and the type to let her husband make all the decisions, was really quite a power behind the scenes of her marriage and her family. She knew what she wanted and she almost always got it. It had been Nura's decision to open an office in San Francisco in the hope that the family could all be together there, instead of the boys in New York and she and their father in the Gulf. She had chosen the new apartment, and now she wanted to choose Rafik's wife for him. That was what concerned Rafik. She wanted to see him married. Not just married, but to Anne. But he too had a strong will, perhaps inherited from his mother, and he had no intention of letting her win the battle of the marriage. It was his life, after all. He just wished he could be a fly on the wall of the tearoom.

There were no flies on any wall of the St. Francis Hotel's tearoom. Everything was sumptuous and luxurious from the thick Oriental carpets to the embossed wall-coverings to the white-jacketed waiters to the woman in the long skirt who played the harp.

Anne was glad she'd worn her one and only suit, and her gloves when the doorman held the door for her and she saw the elegant setting on the first floor. It was a suit she saved for presentations made in front of the teachers' association or on parents' night at school. She noticed that Rafik's mother was wearing an elegant blue silk dress and a hat that set off her silver hair.

She tried to calm the butterflies in her stomach. She knew this was not an ordinary tea. She was going to be asked questions, and she might say the wrong thing or be caught contradicting herself or Rafik. So far she liked the woman very much and she understood that the family as a whole liked her. So what was the real problem? That they liked her *too* much.

Mrs. Harun smiled at her across the room and motioned to her to join her at her small round table.

"What a lovely custom, tea in the afternoon," Nura Harun said. "How kind of you to join me."

Anne murmured that it was her pleasure. Rafik's mother ordered jasmine and Earl Grey tea and sandwiches and cakes. Then she settled back in her chair and surveyed the woman who she surely hoped would be her future daughter-in-law.

"I hope your parents are as happy about your engagement as we are," she said.

Anne murmured something she hoped sounded positive. Mrs. Harun seemed satisfied.

"I hope you'll forgive me for asking some questions," his mother said.

Anne nodded calmly. But inside, her heart was doing flip-flops. What kind of questions? she wanted to ask. But she didn't. She'd find out soon enough.

"Rafik tells me you haven't set a date for the wedding."

"No, no date." That was an easy question and an easy answer. But the woman obviously wasn't finished. It seemed she was just getting started.

"What kind of a wedding do you have in mind?" she asked.

"Well, I'm afraid we haven't discussed it yet," Anne said.

"I see. I'm afraid men are very bad at planning weddings. So if you need any help I would love to step in. Provided your family wouldn't be offended, of course. You see, I have no daughters, only sons. So I have no chance to plan a wedding unless it's for one of the boys."

"I understand."

Fortunately, the small white pots of tea arrived at that moment along with trays of sandwiches: walnut and cucumber, and cream cheese and smoked salmon and chicken salad. The arrival of the food and tea gave Anne an excuse to exclaim over the beautiful presentation. Mrs. Harun poured them each a cup of tea and while they nibbled at the sandwiches any further serious conversation was postponed. Anne would have been happy if it had been canceled completely. But after the sandwiches and before the tarts and cakes, the older woman got down to the subject at hand.

"I thought your friend Carolyn had a lovely church wedding."

"Yes, lovely."

"Would you too be interested in that kind of wedding?" Nura asked very casually.

Anne tried to see herself coming down the aisle at Grace Cathedral as Carolyn had done, preceded by a host of bridesmaids, her husband-to-be and a line of groomsmen at the altar but she knew her wedding—should she marry— would never be as spectacular.

"I think it would be too grand for me," she explained. "I would prefer something at home. I have a garden I'm working on that would be perfect for a wedding. Provided the weather was good and that I'd finished my plantings by then." As soon as she'd said them, she wished she could take back the words. What on earth possessed her to say those things? She'd never consciously thought of her garden as a wedding site before. Never.

Not only that, she was not going to get married any time in the near future. She had no business imagining a wedding anywhere, any time. Still she truthfully couldn't think of a nicer venue than her own backyard. It could be so personal, so private, so intimate, and so romantic. But not at all suitable for a rich sheik. She couldn't share that bit of information with his mother, of course.

"I see," his mother said, setting her teacup in the saucer. "Something small and intimate. It sounds lovely. I wonder...I don't want to impose, but I have a gown that I wore at my wedding. It was designed for me. Of course it wouldn't fit me now, but when I was married I was about your size." Her gaze traveled over Anne's slender figure. "What I mean is that I would be honored if you would wear it. But it is completely up to you. Perhaps you have something in mind already?"

"No, no, nothing," Anne said.

His mother smiled. "It's been in storage, but I could bring it to show you one day. Believe me, I won't be one bit offended if you don't like it or if it doesn't fit you. It's just.... I always wanted to pass it down to someone." There was a wistful tone in her voice Anne couldn't help but notice. It made her feel worse than ever about not marrying her son.

"Thank you," Anne said, touched by the generous offer. "That's very kind of you. I'd love to see it." But she wouldn't be wearing it, she thought. His mother would just have to keep it in storage for a while longer, until one of her sons really decided to get married. That could be years from now or never, she thought. But that was none of her business. The dear woman had no idea how opposed to the idea of marriage her son was and Anne was not going to be the one to tell her.

Apparently satisfied by the way things were progressing in regard to her son's wedding, Nura then changed the subject. Anne was so relieved she was able to relax and happily converse for another hour. Nura Harun was really a very nice person. Because of her background in a foreign country she had many stories to tell, which Anne found fascinating. If Anne ever had a mother-in-law in the future, someone like Rafik's mother would be a good choice. Not that anyone gets to choose her mother-in-law.

After they'd devoured every last crumb of the orange

and currant scones and tiny iced cakes, Anne thanked Mrs. Harun. In front of the hotel his mother kissed her on the cheek and promised they'd get together very soon, and reminded her of the wedding dress.

"Don't feel obligated in any way to wear it," she said. "After all, it may not be your style at all."

Anne assured her she'd love to see it. Before they parted, Nura took Anne's left hand in hers. Looking at her ring finger, she frowned.

"But you have no engagement ring."

"Oh, uh, no, no, not yet." Just when Anne was congratulating herself on escaping from the tea with no consequences, she was caught. She didn't know what to say. They'd never discussed a ring. She always assumed they'd be unengaged before the question came up. But here the question was, rearing its ugly head and leaving her tongue-tied and fumbling for a suitable answer.

"No engagement ring," his mother repeated. She looked thoughtful as she said goodbye and they parted. Anne walked down the street, conscious of her bare ring finger. For the first time in her life, Anne imagined herself wearing a diamond engagement ring and a wedding dress, standing in a leafy arbor like the one in her backyard. She wished the man in her imagination waiting for her at the end of the flagstone path under a trellis didn't have a face and a name. But he did.

Chapter Six

When Rafik picked up Anne to go to her school reception, the first question he asked was about the tea with his mother.

"I had a very nice time," she said, once again enjoying the luxury of the heated seats and the smell of leather in the interior of his sleek foreign sports car.

"So did Mother," Rafik said. "Now she's talking of nothing but the wedding. Did you have to be so agreeable?"

Her mouth fell open in surprise as she turned to look at him. Was he seriously upset? "What did you expect, that I'd be rude and unpleasant?"

"No, of course not," he assured her. "It's not in your nature to be the least bit unpleasant. I don't know what you could have done. I just know that instead of less, there's more pressure than ever on me to get married."

She studied his profile. His forehead was lined with worry, his jaw was clenched. Fortunately he didn't say anything about a ring. Maybe his mother had forgotten all about it. She could only hope so. "Maybe this was a bad idea," she suggested.

"I certainly couldn't have imagined it backfiring," he said dourly.

"If you'd prefer to call it off now, we can turn around and skip this reception."

"Wouldn't that make you look bad?" he asked with a glance in her direction.

"Yes, I suppose it would, but…"

"Then we're going. For all intents and purposes, as far as the rest of the world knows, I'm your fiancé. As for my family, I'll handle them. Now, at your school, is there anything special I'm supposed to tell them?"

"Just act like a responsible and serious man, not like someone who'd carry a female across a hotel lobby on the way to seduce her in his room."

He smothered a smile. "In other words I'm to dispel all notions that I'm some kind of playboy."

"Exactly."

"That shouldn't be a problem."

"Why, because you're such a good actor?" she asked.

"No, because I'm not a playboy anymore." He raised his eyebrows. "Haven't you noticed?"

"Well…"

"I don't hang out in bars anymore, except to meet you. I don't ogle women or attempt to pick them up. I don't even stay up late, not when I have to be in the office by nine. I'm a different person, whether you've noticed or not." He sounded slightly offended that she hadn't noticed, so she tried to reassure him.

"I'm sure you are. But since I didn't really know you before your transformation, you can't blame me for not noticing." She reached over to touch his shoulder as a reassuring gesture and he smiled at her. She smiled back and their eyes met. Her pulse raced. He might not be a playboy anymore, but he hadn't lost his ability to turn women on, especially women like her who hadn't had time to build up a set of defenses against men like him. She withdrew her hand and turned to look out the window to escape the aura around him.

She told herself it was all an act. She warned herself not to get caught up in the act. Because pretending to be Rafik's fiancée, while often stressful, was sometimes enjoyable. If she could call tremors and sudden waves of heat coursing through the body enjoyable sensations. If she didn't mind the dreams involving her and him that interrupted her sleep. She'd been dreaming of her wedding, something she'd never done in her life.

Many girls, such as her friend Carolyn, had been planning their weddings for years, but not Anne. What worried her was that she not only had dreamed of the wedding, but of the honeymoon, too. The honeymoon which took place in a small hotel in some European city with a view over the rooftops and churches and other vaguely famous landmarks. In the dream, they'd close the shutters and tumble back onto the bed where they would make passionate love for hours. She couldn't believe she could even imagine such details. Of how Rafik taught her the secrets of lovemaking. Of how quickly she learned.

She'd wake up in the morning after one of these dreams feeling aware of her body in a way she'd never been before. Her skin was warm and tingly. She had to stand under the shower for many minutes to dispel the notion that she'd actually made love with her husband under a down comforter then eaten croissants and drunk café au lait in bed. She told herself it was just a dream. Where these dreams came from, she couldn't say. She didn't read travel magazines or bride magazines. And she certainly never read those articles with such titles as, "Fifty Ways To Please Your Mate," that she'd seen on the racks in the supermarket.

Since she'd never been to Europe, she wasn't sure which city it was in her dreams. Perhaps it was Paris. She'd taken French in college, and she'd always thought Paris must be the most romantic place in the world. Maybe it was. She would probably never know unless she went along as a chaperone for the older students at her school.

Rafik interrupted these thoughts by asking for directions to the school and Anne started guiltily. The smile on his face made her wonder if he had a way of reading her thoughts. But that was impossible. How could he? Fortunately she didn't worry about him letting her down in front of the faculty and staff of her school. She knew him well enough to know he'd come through for her. What she didn't know was that he had reserves of charm he hadn't even tapped yet, at least not in front of her.

Once inside the ballroom of the sprawling old mansion that made up the centerpiece of the beautiful campus, he made a favorable impression on everyone. He seemed to know just what to say and how long to say it. He asked thoughtful questions, and he answered questions about his background and his business, spending just the right amount of time talking to each person or group of people. He never monopolized the conversation. She didn't think he'd learned that anywhere. It had to be inborn. If she lived to be one hundred, she'd never have his ease in social situations. Together with his looks, it was an unbeatable combination.

Considering it was summer vacation, there was a large crowd gathered, everyone sipping punch, eating cookies and eagerly awaiting a chance to say hello to a genuine, bona fide sheik. Anne knew how surprised they must be to find their quiet, serious first-grade teacher suddenly engaged to an exotic sheik. She could just imagine how many questions they wanted to ask her, such as how had she met him? How long had she known him? How rich was he? Where would they live? and Would she continue to teach?

They did ask some of these questions, excluding the one about how rich he was, of course. She was able to be vague about future plans, but she soon realized how hard it was to skirt around the truth with people she knew so well. She also realized it wasn't going to be quite as easy as she'd thought to explain a broken engagement later. Not when everyone was so happy for her, so delighted with her choice of a man. These thoughts spun around in her mind, and her face hurt from smiling so much.

At one point she was listening to a group of colleagues talk about their fall schedules and Rafik was talking to one of the school's trustees. Listening to his conversation with one ear, she strained to hear what he was saying. She was surprised to hear him talking about his country. About the changes in the last decade, the plans for modernization, the difference between his life and his grandfather's, the old gentleman whose picture she'd seen on the wall of his office. She'd never heard him speak seriously before, and she was impressed with his knowledge and his reverence for the past as well as his enthusiasm for the future. She was so caught up in listening to him, she completely tuned out what her fellow teachers were talking about.

When they asked her a question, she looked blank. They laughed and accused her of being in love. She blushed, and of course she couldn't deny it. She was supposed to be engaged, after all. She tried to explain, but they wouldn't accept her half-hearted explanation. All in all, everyone seemed so happy for her, she didn't argue. Any protest she might make would just make matters worse, so she just let them carry on.

As soon as she could, she excused herself to go to the punch bowl by herself, looking for a few moments to give her mouth a rest from the constant smiling, to cool her overheated skin, gather her thoughts and to try to shake the beginnings of a tension headache. Rafik seemed to be able to carry on forever, but she couldn't. She would never be the social animal he was. Especially when she was pretending to be engaged to a sheik.

At the refreshment table, she ran into Jean Stuart, a teacher who had team-taught a class with her the year before. They'd gotten along so well, Anne was sorry she hadn't kept her promise to keep in touch during the summer.

"Now I know why I haven't heard from you," Jean said with a smile. "You've had other things on your mind."

"But we must get together," Anne said, trying to ignore the mention of "other things."

"In any case, you're still going to the conference this weekend in Monterey, aren't you?" Jean said.

"Of course. And we're rooming together. I'm looking forward to it. Shall we carpool?" Anne asked.

"Good idea. I'll drive," Jean offered. "If you can get along without your fiancé for that long. I'd love to bring Art along, but we couldn't get a baby-sitter. I'm telling you, take advantage of these times while you're young and single and still unencumbered. You look great, you know. Falling in love must agree with you."

Anne didn't know whether to laugh or cry. She had a wild desire to tell her friend the truth. She wondered how she'd endure a whole weekend without spilling the truth. With any luck they'd be talking nonstop about reading techniques and would have no time to discuss personal matters. She also wondered how she could look great when she was living a lie and was worried sick she'd be caught. Fortunately Jean didn't wait for an answer.

"I can see why. Your fiancé is absolutely adorable."

At least she didn't say charming, Anne thought with relief. She was so tired of hearing him described that way. It was even more annoying because he most definitely *was* charming.

"You make a great couple," Jean continued. Just then Rafik glanced over at Anne and winked at her, causing her to blush. Of course, Jean noticed. "What's it like," she asked, "to be in love with a sheik?"

"Oh, well…." Anne said. "It's uh…it's not any different from being in love with anyone else." As if she knew. She'd never been in love with anyone, let alone with Rafik, and he wasn't in love with her. She wondered how they could fool so many people. Everyone here today probably believed them, just as Rafik's family believed them.

"The way you can tell two people are in love," Jean said, as if she'd read Anne's thoughts, "is that their eyes keep meeting. Oh, yes, even though I'm an old married lady, I remember. The thrills, the excitement. No matter where you are, I notice your fiancé always knows where to find you," Jean said. "And you're the same."

Of course she was the same. She had to keep Rafik in her sight in case he needed rescuing from some verbose staff member. As if Rafik needed help in any situation. He moved fluidly from group to group until he ended up at the punch bowl with Jean and Anne. In a moment the headmistress joined them also. So much for Anne's trying to shake her headache. Instead it got worse. She stole a look at her watch and wondered how long they had to stay to be polite.

"I'm so impressed with the faculty and the staff here at

Pinehurst,'' Rafik told the headmistress. ''These are very lucky children who attend this school.''

''If you have children, we would hope to have them enroll here,'' Leona said. ''We have a strong language program for our many international students who go on to study here or abroad.''

Rafik reached for Anne's hand. ''I can't think of a better place for our children, can you?'' he asked her.

Though her hands were cold, her face was flaming. She tried to convey to Rafik with a nudge of her arm and a swift glance that there was no need to carry on about nonexistent children. As skillful in the art of conversation as Rafik was, he could have changed the subject. But he didn't. In fact he pulled Anne close to his side and squeezed her hand, then asked more questions about the preschool program. She wanted to sink through the floor.

''Anne,'' the headmistress said, ''I've unlocked your classroom if you'd like to show it to your fiancé. The painters have finished in there, and I must say it looks quite nice.''

Anne glanced at Rafik. She was sure seeing a first-grade classroom would bore him, though he nodded enthusiastically. But it took what seemed an eternity to get out of the reception. They had to make the rounds once again, thanking everyone for coming and for putting on such a nice party. Anne didn't know what to say when people asked about the wedding. Especially when she was separated from Rafik at the moment. She had no idea what he had been saying about it to everyone. They should have gotten their stories straight before they got here. A small wedding in the far-distant future seemed the safest. That way no one would be expecting their invitations in the mail any time soon, or any time at all.

Finally she and Rafik were alone together outside the

mansion on the front steps. "We don't have to look at the classroom, you know," she said.

"I'd be honored if you'd show it to me," he said. "That way I can picture you at work. After all, you've seen me in my office. Although you perhaps don't have exactly a happy memory of that occasion."

She couldn't deny it. The very thought made her shiver. "I can't imagine what everyone in your office thought of me that day," she said. "Or what conclusions they had drawn. There was your father, your brother, your receptionist... And there I was in my bridesmaid gown and bare feet. Everyone must have been shocked."

"No one, not even Father, ever mentioned it again, and he's pleased about the engagement to say the least, so I guess it didn't hurt your reputation at all. As for mine...I don't think it could have been worse than it was. This engagement has done a lot for it and I have you to thank."

"I thought you were proud of being a playboy."

"Did you?" he asked. They walked in silence down the winding sidewalk from the reception center to the classrooms. "I suppose I was," he said thoughtfully.

The classroom did look good with its freshly painted walls and new carpet. Her desk was back in place along with the little chairs and tables for the students. But the walls were bare and it lacked the warmth and color that only a roomful of six-year-olds and their books and their equipment and her own personal touches could provide.

"Of course it will be more cheerful with posters on the walls and the pictures my students draw."

"I can picture you sitting at your desk with the children sitting quietly, looking at you from their seats, awaiting your instruction," he said.

Anne smiled at the false picture he had of American classrooms. "Actually, they very seldom sit in their seats for very long,'' she explained. ''Sometimes we all sit on the rug and I read a story or we sing a song. They're very lively and restless at this age so I try to keep them busy with a choice of various learning activities. Reading, writing, counting. Last year I set up a play storefront over there in the corner with pretend products and play money. Some children were customers and others clerks. They had a good time and didn't even realize they were doing math.''

''That doesn't sound like the kind of elementary school I went to in my country,'' Rafik said. ''We had individual desks and never got up or spoke without the teacher's permission. Math was learned from a book.''

''Things have changed,'' Anne said, leaning against her desk.

''For the better,'' he said. ''I think it would be an enjoyable experience to be in your class.'' His lips curved in a smile that could only be described as sexy. He must not be aware of the effect it had on her. Of how fast her heart was beating and how the sparks traveled through her body right down to her toes.

''Thank you,'' she said briskly. ''Well, now that you've seen it....'' She couldn't imagine anyone being that interested in a classroom unless they were a student or teacher, but Rafik didn't seem to want to leave. He kept looking around the room and back at her, until finally he was only looking at her. She tried to look away, but she couldn't. The room seemed so small with him in it. He was so big and so out-of-place. He was so far away from her. She felt alone and small. Almost like one of her students. It must be the lack of furnishings or the new paint and the carpet. He kept looking at her. She didn't know what that look in his eyes meant. She just knew she couldn't look away. She also knew she was trembling inside. Before she started trembling on the outside, too, she ran her damp palms against her skirt and started for the door.

"I'd like to come again, when you have your posters up and the art work on the walls...if I may," he said.

"Of course," she said, pushing the door open. "There's an open house in September." By September their false engagement would surely be over and he would have no reason to visit her classroom. For one thing he was probably not sincere, merely expressing his good manners. She didn't know exactly how long this engagement would last, and she didn't want to ask. One of these days it would become clear. It would be over as fast as it had begun. With as little warning. So she'd better be prepared.

When they got to the car, Anne reclined her seat, leaned back and closed her eyes. She was mentally exhausted. But Rafik seemed to be energized.

"You're fortunate to have a nice group of people to work with," he said.

"I know, but it's the children who make it all worthwhile."

"I can see you enjoy your job very much."

She nodded, too tired to speak.

"If we had a wedding, would you be obliged to invite the entire staff?"

She sat up straight and stared straight ahead. "We aren't having a wedding. We aren't even engaged. Remember?"

"Of course I remember," he said.

"I wish you hadn't mentioned our children going to school there." Just saying the words made the heat rush to Anne's cheeks once again.

"What do you mean? Wouldn't you want our children to attend your school?"

"Of course, but we aren't having any children. We aren't

engaged and we aren't getting married." She emphasized each word in turn, as much for him as for herself.

"Obviously you feel quite strongly about it," he said stiffly.

"Don't you?" she asked.

He gave her a long thoughtful look, then opened his mouth to say something, but didn't.

Surely he must know how she felt. How embarrassing it was for her to think of having children with a man who wasn't interested in marriage, either to her or anyone else. A man who could have any woman he wanted. If he wanted to get married, it would certainly be to someone rich and beautiful and socially acceptable. Why not?

"I have to thank you for the wonderful job in there, by the way. But did you have to be so agreeable?" she asked, deliberately mimicking his earlier words.

"Did you expect me to be arrogant and egotistical?"

"No, of course not. It's just that now that they know you, and they obviously like you, everyone will be asking about you and the wedding and you know…"

"Indeed I do know," he said. "It seems that we've unleashed a genie from out of a bottle. We're both in the same situation. For better or for worse."

For better or for worse. The words from the wedding ceremony hung in the air. She didn't know if he knew the significance of them, but she did. She wished she could forget about weddings, especially her own imaginary wedding, but everything and everyone seemed to remind her.

"Anyway it's over," she said. "I won't see any of them until fall, except for Jean who will be at the same conference at Asilomar next weekend."

"You'll be gone all weekend?" he asked, driving down the steep hill on California Street.

"Yes, at a conference center on the beach in Monterey.

It's a secluded spot not many people know about with views of sand dunes and the sound of crashing waves and fireplaces in every room. I'm looking forward to it.''

"Is it only for teachers?" he asked.

"The conference is, but if they're not fully booked the rooms are available to visitors who appreciate the solitude and rustic atmosphere."

"It sounds romantic," Rafik remarked.

"You would think of that," Anne said. She would never admit that she'd thought of it, too. Too many romantic thoughts were in her mind these days. Not to mention those romantic dreams. "But no one will be thinking of romance." Especially not her. Not if she could help it. "We'll be too busy discussing teaching reading to children."

"Do you need a ride down there?" he asked.

"My friend Jean is driving."

"I'll miss you."

"You don't need to say things like that," she said with a frown. "There's no one around to hear."

"I meant it."

She didn't know what to say. He sounded sincere. But why would he miss her? It didn't make sense. He took her home and walked her to the door. He looked as if he was reluctant to leave. He kept making small talk until she took out her key and opened her front door.

"I haven't seen much of the inside of your house," he said. She'd run out to meet him when she heard his car pull up in front of her house earlier that day. The night of the gala, he'd come in to the living room only.

"Yes, I know. If I didn't have a headache, I'd invite you in, but…"

"I didn't mean to force myself on you," he said. "If

you have plans, I understand. You don't have to make up a story about a headache. You can be honest with me."

"Thank you," she said stiffly. "I do have a headache and I am being honest with you. I've told so many lies in the past few days, I couldn't possibly manage another one. Maybe that's why my head hurts. Thanks again." She let herself in and closed the door behind her.

Rafik drove away reluctantly. He had more things to say to Anne. Many more. He had questions to ask her. He felt he scarcely knew her at all. When he'd seen her in her classroom, she seemed to be a different person. Her eyes sparkled and her face glowed when she described her job. He'd always thought her attractive, but she was more than that. The more he got to know her, the more appealing she was. Today she was so beautiful he could hardly take his eyes from her.

He could picture her on the rug with her students gathered around her, their eyes on her as she read to them. How lucky they were to have such a fine teacher as she must be. Just as the headmistress had told him. He wondered how many sides to her personality there were. It seemed he'd have to know her for a long time before he found out. He was envious of Anne's weekend plans. For some reason he felt as if he really *was* engaged and his fiancée was going out of town without him. He knew it didn't make sense, but he felt left out. Now that he was supposed to be engaged he could hardly call other women. Not that he wanted to.

That week he had to endure his mother rhapsodizing about what a wonderful girl Anne was, about the kind of small, garden wedding she wanted and how she was going to try on his mother's wedding dress until he didn't know how much more he could take. Anne had never told him she wanted a garden wedding. Though now that she mentioned it and he'd seen her garden, he had no trouble imagining it. He didn't know why she hadn't told him herself, instead of having to hear it from his mother.

That wasn't all his mother said. She told him that a fiancée needed an engagement ring. She insisted on giving him a ring that had belonged to his grandmother that she thought would be appropriate.

"Although if you want to choose your own..."

"I don't know, Mother. I'll check with Anne."

She pressed the small jeweler's box into his hand. "Just see if she likes it. Your grandmother would be so happy if she knew."

"Yes. All right. Fine," he said, putting the box into his pocket.

At least he could let down his pretenses with his brother, the only one who knew the truth about his engagement.

"How's it going?" Rahman asked on Friday afternoon. "Got a big weekend planned with your *fiancée?*" He grinned at his brother.

Rafik crumpled a sheet of paper and threw it at his brother. "My *fiancée* is going out of town."

"Without you?"

"Yes, without me. She's going to a teacher's conference in Monterey."

"I hear it's a beautiful place," Rahman said. "Sand dunes, crashing surf, sea lions. Why don't you go along?"

"It's for teachers. They'll be doing whatever teachers do. Besides she didn't invite me."

"Since when do you need an invitation to go to Monterey, to book a room at the same place she's staying? Maybe she was too shy to invite you. Maybe she's dying for you to join her there so she can escape all those boring teacher-types. Anyway, she can't be doing her teacher thing every minute, can she?''

"I don't know. What are you doing?''

"Golf tomorrow. Strictly business. A group of investors. Of course if you're not busy, you can join us.''

Rafik had used to like playing golf. But playing with a group of investors sounded dull compared to walking on the sand dunes in Monterey. He knew it wouldn't be very exciting walking there alone. But if he was walking hand in hand with Anne, that was a different story. It shouldn't be impossible if they were both staying at the same place.

He pictured her hair curling in damp tendrils in the ocean spray, her cheeks pink from the breeze off the sea. His brother was right. He didn't need an invitation to visit Monterey. If he ran into Anne while he was there, it would be a coincidence. He'd soon get the hint if she didn't want him around, in which case he would tactfully disappear back to his room with his own fireplace where he would read various prospectuses from his briefcase which were piling up on his desk.

He couldn't get the image of the wood-burning fireplace in the rustic cabin out of his mind. If he really had a fiancée it would be only normal for them to spend a weekend together on the ocean, making love in the cabin in front of the flickering flames. But with Anne, who was not only *not* his fiancée, but a virgin to boot…there was no chance. Maybe it was time he found a real fiancée. On the other hand, the last time he had had a real fiancée, it had been a disaster. His parents had been thrilled, just as they were now, for a while. He'd been happy, too—at least he'd thought he was. Until it ended.

But he hadn't known the woman. He'd just thought he had. When she'd walked out, taking his ring and his joie de vivre and his trust with her, he'd sworn he'd never do it again. Never fall in love, never get engaged and never, never get married. He still felt the same. But that had nothing to do with his urge to see Anne this weekend in a different setting. He couldn't get the image out of his mind: the wind in her hair, her cheeks glowing from the walk on the beach…

"I don't know, Rahman. I'm in a tough spot. I'm not really engaged, but I have to act as if I am. I can't play the field, but I don't have the benefits of a real fiancée either." He ran his hand through his hair.

"Well, you have the parents off your back."

"Hah. Now they're pressuring me to get married. And it's all your fault. This was your idea, remember? Why don't you get engaged? That would distract them."

"Sure, if I could find someone like Anne, I might think about it. But I suspect she's one in a million. Sweet, high-spirited…"

"Kind, beautiful, smart, sexy…" Rafik murmured.

"What was that?" Rahman asked.

Rafik got out of his swivel chair. "Nothing. Enough of this. I've got some phone calls to make. See you later."

"Wait a minute. How much later? Are you going to take my advice? Where are you going?"

"Nowhere." He put one hand on his brother's shoulder and ushered him to the door and closed it behind him. Outside he could hear Rahman protesting.

"You can't get rid of me so easily," Rahman complained from the other side of the door. "Answer my questions. I'm your brother."

Rafik laughed quietly and picked up the phone.

Chapter Seven

Instead of having his secretary do it, Rafik made the reservation at the conference center himself. They asked if he was a part of the teachers' group, he said no. He was afraid they'd say they were booked up, but they found an ocean-view cottage for him, only steps from the beach. He wanted to ask how far that was from Anne's lodgings, but he didn't. At the hotel in the city where he was staying along with Rahman until they found an apartment, he packed his bag. Tossing casual slacks and sweaters into a duffel bag, he felt more excited than he had any right to be. He told himself she might not be happy to see him. She might not have time to see him. He told himself it didn't matter. He was seeing a part of the state he hadn't seen before. But what he wanted was to see a part of Anne he hadn't seen before.

Of course, he'd seen quite a bit, considering she was a virgin and she wasn't engaged to him at all. But he wanted more. He wanted to break down her reserves. He wanted to know how she really felt about him. But what if she asked the same thing of him? What would he say? He didn't know. He only knew his feelings were changing by the day, by the minute. Every meeting with her revealed a new layer of her personality. It was like peeling an onion. He'd only just begun, and he didn't want to stop.

What else did he want? He couldn't deny he wanted to make love to her. There was a chemistry between them; there had been since he'd first set eyes on her at his cousin's wedding. She wasn't his type, he'd known that from the beginning also. That didn't stop him from pursuing her. She must feel the attraction, too, no matter how hard she tried to put him off. He couldn't be the only one. But he didn't know if she'd continue to resist him. Or how far he would go, knowing she was a virgin.

He left on Friday afternoon, choosing to drive on Highway One, taking the scenic route south from San Francisco. He thought about calling Anne before he left, but he was afraid if he told her his plans, she'd express surprise and no pleasure. He didn't know what he'd do then. He could go anyway or stay home. This way if she didn't want him there, it would be too late. She'd have to deal with his presence, unless she just ignored him. He didn't like that idea and he had no contingency plan, unless it was to walk the dunes by himself, a lonely figure tramping about in the mist, which might encourage her to feel somewhat sympathetic toward him. But he couldn't count on that.

He didn't know what route Anne and her friend had taken, but he wished she was with him to share the ride, to share the view of the sun glittering on the vast blue ocean. He'd point out how the ocean seemed to stretch forever to the horizon. He loved seeing her face light up with pleasure at something simple, like the joys of her garden.

One of the reasons he was on his way to Monterey was

to watch the changing expressions on her face. He'd seen the delight at her garden, despair at her predicament with her school, disgust at his teasing, and mixed emotions as sexual awareness crept up on her and threatened to overwhelm her at the gala ball. He was aware that her face might not light up at the sight of him arriving to interfere with her plans for the weekend. He could only hope if she wasn't exactly happy to see him, she'd at least be polite. Of course she would be. That was Anne.

When he arrived at the sprawling, low, brown-shingled conference buildings, he parked his car and was shown to his cottage through the trees. It was everything he'd imagined, and completely different from any other weekend retreat he'd been to. The cabin was outfitted with a king-sized bed covered with a down comforter. There were native blankets hung on the walls and handwoven rugs on the floor. The fire was laid in the fireplace and the view of the dunes and the ocean from his window was spectacular. This was California, a different California than he'd seen. Now, if only he had someone to share it with. Someone special. Like his fiancée.

Anne was walking through the fir trees from her cabin to the main lobby where the welcome reception was being held before dinner. Passing the parking lot she noticed a low-slung black sports car, and she stopped in her tracks and stared at it. Her heart thudded wildly, though she tried to dismiss the reason. There were many sports cars in California. She just hadn't noticed this one when they'd arrived an hour ago. She didn't know much about sports cars. She couldn't tell the difference between a Porsche and a BMW unless she looked at the logo, but this car looked familiar. It couldn't be his, of course, because Rafik was in San Francisco.

She took a deep breath and continued walking. Inside the lounge, she pinned a name tag on her sweater and refastened the clip in her hair that the wind had loosened, then proceeded to make the rounds of the room, greeting old friends from previous conferences and introducing herself to people she didn't know. It was the kind of gathering where, though she didn't know everyone, she was at ease. These were her colleagues from around the greater Bay Area. She would have been even more at ease if she didn't have the nagging feeling that it was just remotely possible that Rafik was here somewhere.

Because of this feeling, she found herself losing her train of thought in the middle of a conversation. She found herself looking out the large picture windows at the dunes in the dusk, as if he might be sauntering by, his collar up against the cold air, his black hair blown back in the wind. But of course he wasn't. He was back in San Francisco. She had no idea what he was doing. She hadn't asked him. She'd just figured it was none of her business. Of course if he were her fiancé, it would be her business. If he were her fiancé, he might be there with her, waiting in the cottage, a fire burning, a bottle of wine chilling.... She dismissed these ridiculous thoughts from her mind.

The next event was a family-style dinner followed by a short welcoming speech from the president of the teachers' association, who handed out a packet of materials and a schedule of the weekend's activities. Anne gathered her materials and put them into her book-bag. Though she had no reason to think so, she had a funny feeling she was being watched.

She glanced out the huge windows into the darkness and saw nothing. There was nothing to see in the dark. She put her jacket on, then made her way back to her cottage by the lighted pathways. She sniffed the air, redolent with pine and fir, and resolved not even to glance toward the parking lot. Sports cars all looked the same, no matter who owned them, especially in the dark.

"Hello, Anne."

Her heart pounded erratically at the sound of his voice. She stopped walking, frozen in place. The voice came from the darkness a few feet ahead of her, and in a moment he appeared, his hair wind-tossed and his face half in shadows.

"Rafik, what are you doing here?"

"I wanted to get some fresh air," he said, "and a change of scenery. Besides, the city was dull and boring without you."

She almost laughed at this flimsy excuse. "I can't imagine you bored in the city just because I wasn't there. How did you get along for thirty-some years without me?"

"I don't know," he said solemnly. "But it's beautiful here, just as you said. And I'm glad I came."

"Are you staying here?" She looked around, staring at the dark shapes of the trees, still in shock at the idea of Rafik here in Monterey. If she'd thought she couldn't picture him in a rustic setting like this because he was always so perfectly groomed and so citified, she was wrong. Because now that he was here, in a thick, Irish fisherman's sweater that appeared to have been knitted especially for him, he seemed to fit in as much as anyone. So far she'd seen him at a formal wedding reception, in his office, at a gala ball, a school function, in her garden and now this. In each setting, he seemed as at ease as if he'd been born to it. Probably, like a chameleon, he would be equally at ease in a tent in the desert or in the palace of a sheik.

"Despite the fact that you teachers are taking up much of the grounds, they luckily had an empty cottage for me," he said in answer to her question. He took her book-bag out of her hand as if it were way too heavy for a fragile thing like her and it was the most natural thing in the world that he should carry her belongings. He tucked her arm in his as if she belonged to him.

She stifled the urge to pull her arm away and say she could manage by herself. But she restrained herself. After all, he'd come all this way to…to do what? Breathe some fresh air? Escape from boredom? See her? Not likely. She didn't know what to think.

"You shouldn't be out here by yourself in the dark," he said. "Where's your friend?"

"Jean? She left the meeting early tonight. Her husband is with her. He decided at the last minute to come and enjoy the surroundings." Left unsaid was that he'd decided to enjoy his wife in these bucolic surroundings—the romantic fireplace, the giant bed and the freedom from his work schedule and from their kids. Anne had seen the sparkle in her friend's eyes when she'd told her about the change in plans.

"I hope you don't mind, Anne," Jean had said. "We don't get away from the kids together very often. Art found a baby-sitter so he could come along. I figure I won't be busy every minute and…well, we'll have some quality time together, just the two of us." She could have sworn Jean blushed at the word *quality*. Knowing Jean had been married for some years and had two children, Anne was impressed to find romance was on her friend's mind. And on her husband's.

"Wasn't she to be your roommate?" Rafik asked.

"That's right. But her husband also booked a cabin. She gained a husband for the weekend, but I lost a roommate."

"Too bad," he said. But he didn't sound like he thought it was too bad. "Then I'll see you back to your cabin."

"Thank you, but…" But what? She couldn't think of any excuse why he shouldn't walk her back to her cabin.

This time she wouldn't be as rude as she'd been when he'd walked her to her front door and she'd refused to let him come in. That time he would have invaded her private space. Her room here wasn't really hers. It couldn't hurt for him to come in for a moment for a cup of coffee made from the little complimentary packets and small coffee-maker provided by the management.

He didn't hesitate when she issued the invitation. Perhaps he remembered what had happened last time, when she'd almost closed the door in his face. She was surprised to find a bottle of wine propped up against her door with a note from Jean which she read out loud.

"Sorry to wimp out on you, Anne. Here's a bottle of wine for company. It's not as old as I am, but enjoy! See you at the morning session."

"How thoughtful of your friend," Rafik said. He quickly made himself at home in her cabin, lighting the fire in the fireplace while she poured the water into the coffeemaker.

"Shall I open the wine?" he asked. "Or are you taking your antihistamines?"

She blushed at the memory of the last time she'd combined alcohol with allergy medicine. "Go ahead," she said. "I should be able to handle a glass of wine tonight."

"If you pass out, at least you'll be close to your bed," Rafik said, with a pointed glance at the large bed that seemed to dominate the room.

"I won't pass out, I promise you," Anne said, determined to look anywhere but at the bed. "I learned my lesson. Pills or alcohol, but not both at the same time. I'll never forget—"

"—sleeping with me?" he asked with a gleam in his eye as he poured some wine into a water glass for her.

"I don't remember that part," she said stiffly. There he went, teasing her again. She didn't know if she'd ever get over having spent the night in bed with a stranger. Or if she'd ever be able to handle his teasing. "I suppose most of the women who sleep with you never forget it," she countered.

"I don't know about that," he said. "I can only say it was an unusual beginning for a relationship."

"A relationship?" she asked. "Is that what we have?"

He handed her a glass of wine. "What do you call it?" he asked. "Sometimes I feel like we're really engaged, other times like I'm just getting to know you."

She didn't know what to say to that. She was just getting used to the idea of him being there, in her room, when he lifted his glass to hers.

"Here's to getting to know you better," he said in a low voice that was so full of suggestions it sent a chill through her body, though her skin was burning. "Come here by the fire," he said, as if he felt she needed to warm up. They sat next to each other on the soft carpet, legs stretched out toward the fire, shoulders touching. It was all so natural, so comfortable, and yet there was an electric current of excitement in the air. She didn't know what was going to happen next. She kicked off her loafers and curled her toes in anticipation of what she didn't know. She noticed Rafik had left his shoes at the door, perhaps an Arabian custom.

"I didn't come here for the scenery or the fresh air," he said solemnly, setting his wineglass on the hearth. "I came because of you."

She tried to say something, but her throat was clogged with emotion. She wanted to believe him. She didn't know why he'd lie about something like that, but she was afraid to believe him, too.

"I've never felt this way before," he said, taking her hand in his and massaging her palm with his thumb. "I've been thinking about you all the time. When I'm not with you, I miss you. I want to know where you are and what you're doing. You're different from every woman I've ever known. You have me wrapped around your finger.'' He brought her hand to his lips and kissed her index finger. ''This one.''

His touch sent her pulse hammering. She turned to meet his gaze in the flickering firelight. His voice reached deep down into her and touched her as she'd never been touched before. Something inside her melted and flowed and threatened to overwhelm her. If she could have found her voice, she would have told him she'd never wrapped anyone around her finger. If he didn't look so serious, so sincere and so genuine, she would have doubted him.

He leaned toward her and framed her face with his strong fingers. She knew he was going to kiss her. She wanted it more than anything she'd ever wanted before. She wanted him to kiss her and never stop. She wanted him to brand her with his kiss. She wanted him to claim her for his own, though rationally she knew it would never happen. She was not thinking rationally. This time it was not the wine. She'd barely had time for one sip. She was under his spell. Under the spell of his voice and his dark eyes and his overwhelming presence. She didn't know what he was waiting for. She was ready. She was beyond ready. She was desperate. If he didn't kiss her soon, she'd have to—

When his lips finally met hers she sighed in the back of her throat and gave in to the sensations that rushed through her body. The heat that suffused her limbs spread and invaded her core. Frightened by her own reaction, she pulled back and reached awkwardly for her wineglass. ''This might be better if I had a little more to drink,'' she said.

He shook his head. ''This time I want you to know exactly what's happening,'' he said. ''Because last time...'' He didn't finish his sentence. Instead, he pressed his lips against her neck, under her ear where her pulse beat rapidly.

"Don't remind me," she breathed.

"That was then," he whispered in her ear. "This is now."

He kissed her again. This time his mouth was hot and heavy and demanding. This time she didn't even think about pulling back. She was no longer afraid of her own reaction. She was only afraid he'd stop too soon. She met his kiss with one of her own, just as hot and just as intense as his. He moaned low in his throat and pulled her to him so her breasts were pressed against his hard chest. He tangled his hand in her hair and removed the clip that fell onto the carpet.

The heat from the fire and the heat that built inside her set her body on fire. She struggled to remove her sweater, knowing she was wearing a turtleneck shirt underneath. But somehow Rafik was helping her out of both garments, tossing them aside and then gazing at her in rapt admiration. Her breasts ached and her nipples budded under his gaze. She'd never been so aware of her body before. Never knew it could feel this way.

"You are so beautiful," he said reverently, lifting one lacy bra strap to kiss her shoulder, trailing kisses to the valley between her breasts. Her body responded as if she'd been touched by a live wire. She felt as if the blood in her veins had turned to molten lava. She shuddered from the sheer ecstasy of his mouth on her tender skin.

"Your skin is like delicate porcelain," he murmured. "I want to kiss every inch from your head to your toes. I want you, Anne. I want you so much it hurts. I think I have since the first moment I saw you. If I had the chance I'd make love to you in a way you'd never forget. Sweetly, tenderly, passionately. Tell me if you feel the same. If you want what I want.''

She gazed into his eyes, her skin burning, her whole body throbbing with desire. She could imagine what a gentle considerate lover he would be. How he could awaken in her such passion as she had only heard about. ''Yes,'' she breathed. ''Oh, yes, but…'' But she knew she couldn't do this. She knew that no matter how she felt about Rafik he was the same playboy he had been the first moment she'd seen him. He didn't want a fiancée then and he didn't want one now. Not really.

He didn't want to get married. He might never get married. And if he did, it wouldn't be to her. It would be to one of those sophisticated women she'd seen at the gala ball. The only reason one of them wasn't playing the role of his fiancée was that he hadn't asked them. The thought of Rafik with another woman made her so sad a tiny tear sprang to her eye and trickled down her cheek.

''What is it?'' he asked anxiously. ''What have I said to make you cry?''

She reached for her shirt and pulled it on over her head. She took her sweater and put it on over her shirt. ''Nothing. It's nothing you said. It's what you are.''

''What I am? What am I?'' he asked, his eyebrows drawn together in a puzzled frown.

With her shirt on and her sweater in her hand, she inched away from him on the carpet though she wanted to stay in his arms more than anything she'd ever wanted before. She wanted him to make love to her all night long. She wanted to learn the sensual secrets only he knew. She wanted him to awaken her to every physical pleasure in the world. But that was not going to happen, even though every iota of her being was demanding to know why she was stopping what could be the most incredible, most unforgettable night of her life.

Somewhere a voice inside her was telling her she might never have another chance like this. She was in romantic surroundings with a man she could fall in love with if she had half a chance. A man she was in very great danger of falling in love with in spite of everything she knew about him.

It was not going to happen because, despite these feelings, Anne had learned long ago to protect herself from being hurt. Her instincts told her that this man could hurt her more than she'd ever been hurt before, if she let him. If she let him, he'd make mad, passionate love to her and be gone in the morning. Or if he wasn't gone in the morning, he would be gone sometime in the future.

Some day very soon he'd be gone from her life, despite the fact that his family approved of her, that his mother wanted her to wear her wedding dress and despite the fact that there was a physical attraction between them. An attraction that heightened her awareness of him and of herself every time she was in his presence. When he looked at her she felt faint. When he touched her she thought she might burn up. She reminded herself that Rafik was not going to marry her. She had to keep that simple fact in mind at all times. Because if she forgot, she was in terrible danger. His question hung in the air.

What am I?

She got to her feet and stumbled to the edge of the bed, where she sat looking down at him. She owed him an answer. She owed him an explanation for misleading him into thinking she'd make love to him tonight or ever.

"You're a sheik, for one thing," she said, elbows on her knees, resting her chin in her hands.

He smiled. "Surely you don't hold that against me."

"You're a sheik," she repeated, "you're rich and you have everything you want. I'm a schoolteacher. I work for a living. Everything I want I must earn."

"You make me sound like a spoiled brat," he said. "I, too, work for a living," he insisted.

"Of course, I didn't mean... What I meant was that I'm not in your league."

"No one cares about that," he said.

"I care," she said. "I told you I was a virgin. You asked me why and I told you it was partly for lack of opportunity. Now I know that isn't the whole story. I know now that even given the opportunity to lose my virtue, I will remain a virgin until I marry. I want to marry someone who respects me, who loves me and who appreciates me."

"But, Anne, I respect you and I appreciate you, more than you know."

She nodded sadly. She noticed he hadn't said he loved her because he didn't. At least he was honest. He hadn't said he'd marry her either, but that was not a surprise.

"I know you do," she said. "And I also know I don't know if I'll ever find anyone who will offer me what you have tonight. But I know I'm not going to make love with anyone until I find that person, the person I'm going to spend the rest of my life with."

Rafik's face was a display of disappointment. His eyes were dark pools of sadness. "And if you don't?" he asked.

"If I don't, it won't be the end of the world," she said. "I have a life. I never went around looking for a man to marry and I never will. I never felt unfulfilled. I never yearned for a man to complete my life either. If it happens, it happens." She was proud of how level her voice was, how calm she sounded when inside she was a mass of contradictions.

Her body was still on fire, she ached for Rafik to make

love to her. She knew deep down she might never have another chance, and this saddened her more than she'd ever let him know. She also knew she was right. And this certainty gave her the courage to call a halt to his lovemaking and tell him how she felt.

He got slowly to his feet. For the first time since they'd met she thought he looked uncertain as to what to do next. Whether to stay or whether to go. He looked as if he wanted to say something, to try to persuade her to change her mind. He looked as though he wanted to stay but knew he must leave. After a long, searching look at her face, he seemed to make his decision.

"I'll say good-night then," he said, his voice slightly uneven. "I hope I haven't spoiled your weekend. It's the last thing I wanted to do."

He didn't say what the first thing he'd wanted to do was, but she thought she knew. He'd come to make love to her. She was flattered, disturbed, excited, let-down and sad all at the same time. She didn't get up to see him to the door. She didn't trust her legs to support her. She buried her face in her hands and didn't look up until she heard the door close softly. Then he was gone.

She didn't sleep well that night. She wondered if he did. She tossed and turned, as erotic images of what might have been played across her mind like an X-rated movie. She knew she'd made the right decision, but she couldn't banish the doubts. Couldn't deny the voice in her mind that told her she might never have another chance. That she might go to her grave a virginal spinster schoolteacher. She'd told Rafik she'd never gone around looking for someone to marry. Never yearned for a man in her life or felt unfulfilled. But that was then. This was now. She was not the same person who'd met a sheik at a wedding some weeks ago.

She now knew what she was missing. She knew that Rafik had opened up a whole new world to her. A world of feelings and emotions she'd never experienced before. Or if she'd felt them, she'd kept them under wraps. She had no idea that her body could respond the way it had, so strongly that she almost gave in to temptation. That didn't change anything. It didn't change the fact that he wasn't in love with her and even if he had been, he had no intention of marrying her.

The next morning, she was full of resolve not to let Rafik spoil her weekend. She hoped he'd gone home, but if he hadn't, that was up to him. It had nothing to do with her. She was determined to get as much out of the conference as possible. She walked briskly along the winding path to the main center for the continental breakfast.

Her friend Jean caught up with her on the path. "How was it?" she asked.

Anne stared at her for a long moment. Did she know? Had she seen Rafik leaving her cabin? "Fine. Oh, the wine. It was great. Thank you so much."

"I hated to leave you in the lurch like that."

Anne was determined not to say a word about Rafik, the less said about his visit the better. Especially now that she realized Jean didn't know he was there. Or had been there. She could only hope he'd gone back to San Francisco. But he hadn't. He came up behind them, announcing himself with a cheerful good morning. Anne caught her toe and stumbled on the pavement. Her heart leaped almost to her throat.

"How are you ladies this morning?" he asked.

Jean turned and her mouth fell open in surprise. All three of them stopped to exchange greetings. Anne knew it was the only thing to do, though every instinct told her to run.

She even had enough composure to ask Jean if she remembered Rafik and reintroduce him.

"Remember him? How could I forget?" Jean asked. Then she turned to Rafik. "What are you doing here?" she asked. Then she chuckled. "As if I didn't know. Anne, you devil, you never said a word."

Fortunately Rafik knew what to say, because Anne was tongue-tied. "It was a surprise," Rafik said. "She didn't know I was coming. Neither did I until the last minute."

"You should have told me," Jean chided them both. "Do you play golf? Because Art is going to Pebble Beach this morning and he's looking for a partner."

Rafik assured her he did play golf and would be delighted to join her husband at one of the famed Pebble Beach golf courses. He turned around and went off to connect with Jean's husband so they could make plans.

"What a surprise," Jean said with a sideways glance at Anne after Rafik had left. "No wonder you look like you haven't slept a wink."

Anne gulped. How could she answer that? She couldn't. All she could do was to smile enigmatically. Fortunately some other teachers joined them and that was the end of any more talk about Rafik. But not the end of Anne's thoughts about him. If only he'd left early that morning. Or better yet, last night. Now he was playing golf today and heaven only knew when he'd leave for good. She couldn't go through another evening like last evening. She thought Rafik was sensitive enough not to want to either.

The day dragged by. Though the sessions were interesting, Anne couldn't concentrate. She couldn't stop thinking of Rafik, wondering what his plans were and how he felt about last night. She hoped she hadn't hurt his feelings. She hoped when he thought it over, he'd realize why she'd said no. Why she was saving herself for marriage. She hoped he didn't think she'd led him on, then changed her mind.

After the last workshop, Anne avoided Jean. She didn't want to have to explain anything to her. Didn't want to answer any questions about their plans for the evening in case she suggested the four of them get together. She hoped Rafik would go home, then she could explain that he had business to attend to and couldn't stay any longer.

Anne made a quick trip to her cabin to grab her jacket, determined to enjoy a walk on the beach by herself while she had the chance. Fortunately there was neither a note pinned to the door nor a bottle of wine on the porch. She hoped she'd be alone tonight. She'd build her own fire and sit there watching the flames by herself. She might be lonely, but lonely was better than losing her virtue to a man who had seduction and not marriage on his mind. She hoped Rafik would be far away by then. But would he be far from her thoughts? She had to make an effort to banish him to the periphery of her consciousness where he belonged. Some day he'd be gone altogether from her life, but not quite yet.

She headed out onto a rickety boardwalk through the ice plant toward the dunes. The wind blew; the sun shone its last rays on the shimmering water. She needed the cold air to blow away her problems and soothe her anguished psyche. There were a few other people on the beach, some walking their dogs, a few couples arm in arm as they trudged through the sand.

But as dusk fell, she kept her head down and didn't see anyone. Her thoughts were filled with ways of getting out of this awkward arrangement with Rafik. She wondered when and how they could break off the engagement. It couldn't happen any too soon for her. Surely, after last night Rafik must be feeling the same.

She was so wrapped up in her worries, she didn't realize how far she'd walked or how late it was until she looked at her watch. Only then did she turn around and start back. Instead of walking, she jogged. The cold air filled her lungs, and she was glad she'd come out this evening. The exercise took her mind off her problems. It might be hard going, plodding through the sand, but she ought to do this more often. She needed to get out and run. It was good for the body and good for the soul, too. If you pushed yourself to the limits, you couldn't worry about a little thing like a false engagement.

She continued to congratulate herself on her newfound love of exercise until she stumbled over a large piece of driftwood and twisted her ankle. She gasped in pain and fell forward, bracing herself with her hands, as she landed on the sand. She lay there panting. When she caught her breath she touched her ankle and jumped as the pain shot through the bone. She sat with her legs stretched out in front of her staring at her feet. With an effort, she got to her knees and told herself to get up and walk. But she couldn't. She fell back onto her rear, realizing her ankle was not going to support her. After only a few minutes it had swollen to the size of a tennis ball.

Tears of frustration filled her eyes. She felt foolish and stupid. She'd come too far. She hadn't told anyone where she was going. She hadn't paid attention to the time or the distance. She'd been thinking of Rafik. It was all his fault. Gingerly she touched her ankle again, thinking she'd been a wimp. It might not be so bad. It might even be getting better. She ran her fingers over the lump, hoping the swelling had gone down, but it hadn't. The tears ran down her cheeks. She sobbed.

She told herself crying would not help. She couldn't just lie there crying like a baby. She had to do something. Like call for help. She swallowed hard, then she called for help over and over. But no one heard. No one came. She yelled until her voice was hoarse. She crawled across the sand, dragging her sore ankle behind her until she finally stopped to rest. She wouldn't give up. Even though at this rate it would take all night to get back to the conference center. It didn't matter. She had to do it. She forced herself to move. Sand blew into her ears, sifted into her mouth and grated her skin.

She took a deep breath and tried again. "Help, help! Anybody. Please help me. Rafik. Rafik. Where are you?"

She was cold. She'd never been so cold. The wind went right through her windbreaker and the sweater she wore. She had visions of hot chocolate, of a warm fire. But the vision she couldn't dismiss was Rafik. Rafik trudging across the dunes to rescue her. That's when she knew she must be hallucinating.

Chapter Eight

Rafik spent a pleasant day on the golf course with Jean's husband. He had learned to play as a boy in his country at a club where the course was made of rough greenery and watered with recycled water. As usual, he and his brother had kept up a friendly rivalry in golf, digging holes in the sand for a makeshift putting green at the family compound. They competed in golf as they did in all sports, from touch football to sailing races in the Gulf waters, and as they did in life in general. Rafik managed to keep up a friendly conversation with Jean's husband while his mind was on Anne and the events of last night.

He'd certainly misjudged Anne. Even worse, he'd misjudged himself. He'd thought he could seduce her. He'd thought he could seduce anyone he wanted. He always had in the past. Also he felt sure she wanted him as much as he wanted her. The strange part was, she probably did, but her scruples prevented her from doing anything about it. He'd never run into anyone like her before.

He respected her for that. She was saving herself for

marriage. He wondered what kind of a man she'd marry when she did marry. He had no doubt she'd marry. She was everything a man wanted. A man who wanted to get married, that is. She was sweet and beautiful and sexy and smart, too. Even Rahman had noticed.

She wouldn't marry a sheik. She'd made that quite clear. That decision didn't hurt his feelings. Not at all. She was entitled to her opinion that sheiks were rich and spoiled. He had to admit that comparatively speaking, he was rich. Maybe he was spoiled, too. He had everything he wanted. Except for Anne. She wasn't available except for marriage. It was frustrating, but he thought he'd better get used to the idea, because if ever he saw determination in anyone's eyes or heard it in their voice, it was last night in her room when she'd told him in no uncertain terms that she wasn't interested in an affair with him.

As soon as he saw her he'd tell her he understood, and he wished her the best. Then he'd call off the engagement. He'd make up some story for his family and let her get on with her life. There was no reason for her to waste any more time on him. Before he walked out of her life, he wished for two things. The first was impossible—that he could make love to her—and the second was faintly possible; he wanted to show her he wasn't the selfish spoiled rich brat she took him for.

He was so engrossed in his plans for the future, he let Jean's husband win the game, something he never would have permitted, not without a battle, in his past matches. Losing would have bothered the old, competitive Rafik. Now he just didn't seem to care all that much. Jean's husband bought him a beer in the clubhouse after the game, and it was almost dark as they drove back.

In the car, as they passed the manicured greens on one side of the highway and the dark blue bay on the other, Art

told him how much he was looking forward to spending
the evening with his wife. His eyes brightened when he
talked about his two children, and he remarked on what a
rarity it was to get his wife alone for the weekend, at least
part of the weekend. When they parted in the parking lot,
Rafik felt almost envious. Those cabins with their big fireplaces and huge beds covered with down quilts were made
for making love. But not for him. Not tonight. And not
ever with Anne.

He was practicing his speech as he walked to Anne's
cabin, about how much he respected her and understood
her position. But when he got there he could see it was
dark inside, and there was no response when he knocked.
He went to Jean and Art's cabin to ask about her, but she
wasn't there. Jean said she hadn't seen her since that afternoon. He strode briskly to the main building, a slight
feeling of apprehension nagging him.

Maybe the sessions had gone on late, or maybe she was
lingering over coffee, talking to friends. But the session was
over and there were only a few teachers gathered in informal discussions. He asked them if they knew where she
was, but they didn't even know her. One suggested that he
check the beach. She'd seen someone in a jacket pass by
the window an hour or so ago heading up the beach.

Rafik frowned. It was dark out there. The moon was
nowhere to be seen. If she'd gone for a walk, she'd be back
by now. Unless something had happened. A wave washing
her out to sea. An encounter with a rabid animal. He
shrugged off such preposterous ideas, but he couldn't get
rid of the worry that nagged him. He pushed open the heavy
door to the deck and stood there listening to the pounding
surf for a moment. The wind howled in the cypress trees
and whistled across the sand. He had a choice. He could
go back to his cabin and pace up and down and wait for

her to call him. After all, she might have found a ride and gone back to the city. No matter how she felt about him, he didn't really think she'd go without telling him. So he had no choice really. He had to try to find her.

His mind was full of images. Anne on a cliff, washed out to sea by a huge wave. Anne tossed about by an angry sea. Anne surrounded by sharks. Or Anne being torn to shreds by mad dogs on the beach. He walked faster and faster until he was running. He thought he was running, but the wind pushed him back, the sand pulled at his feet and dragged him back. He wondered if he was making any progress at all.

"Anne. Anne." When he called her name, the wind tore the words from his mouth and swallowed them up. It was so dark he could only see a few feet ahead of him. He stopped and stood on the wet sand staring out to sea. He could see nothing, hear nothing but the roar of the ocean.

He plowed into the wind again, calling her name until he was hoarse. He had no idea how far he'd come, but he imagined he could hear her voice. He wanted to hear it so badly he thought he did hear it. He crisscrossed the beach and then he saw her, sprawled out on the sand. His heart thudded. She had to be all right, she had to. If anything had happened to her…

He bent down and lifted her up in his arms. She clung to him like a limpet clinging to a rock. He could feel her heart beating steadily through her jacket. A rush of relief filled his body.

"Rafik," she mumbled. "You came. I knew you would."

"Of course I would," he said, pressing her close to him. "What happened?"

"My ankle. I fell. I can't walk."

"It's okay. I'll carry you." He shifted her in his arms.

She wrapped her arms around his neck, and he plowed forward. It wasn't easy to make his way through the drifting sand, but at least he had the wind at his back this time. She buried her face in his sweater and didn't say a word.

"Are you all right?" he asked.

"Cold," she said. He held her even tighter. She wasn't heavy, it was his legs that felt too heavy to lift them up and take step after step. His heart was pounding from the effort. He wanted to sit down and rest, but he was afraid she might be suffering from hypothermia, and he had to get her back.

After an eternity, when his legs felt like lead and he thought he couldn't make them move forward another step, and his arms were numb, he saw the lights from the cottages of the conference center.

"We're back. We made it," he told her.

She murmured something incoherent.

He turned up the path and headed for his cabin. Still holding her with one arm, he extracted his key from his pocket and shoved the door open. He set her on the bed and collapsed next to her. Suddenly he remembered that night at the hotel. He remembered trying to wake her up, undressing her, sleeping next to her. He was enormously relieved when she sat up on the bed and sighed loudly.

"You had me worried," he said, staring at her with disbelief. It all seemed like a bad dream—her being lost and hurt. His worst fears were almost realized. "I thought you might have been swept out to sea or…or attacked. Thank God I found you. What happened?"

"I went for a walk on the beach. I wasn't thinking about where I was going and suddenly it was dark. I decided to run back and I tripped over something. I think it was driftwood. I tried to walk, but I couldn't. My ankle just wouldn't work. I dragged myself for a while then I gave up. It's this ankle," she said, stretching her leg out in front of her. "I think I sprained it."

"Let me see." Very gently he removed her shoe and sock and held her foot in his hand. "That doesn't look good," he said, observing the huge reddened lump on her ankle. He took off her other sock and shoe to compare her ankles.

"Look," he said. "It's huge. You need to see a doctor. Just to make sure nothing's broken."

"Not now," she said. "I don't want to go anywhere." She leaned back against the pillows and closed her eyes.

"Of course you won't go anywhere," he said. "We'll get someone to come here."

"I'm sure I'll be fine in the morning," she assured him. "Anyway, doctors don't make house calls anymore."

"You let me worry about that. In the meantime we follow the first aid instructions—Rest, Ice, Compression and Elevation." First he turned the thermostat up to high. Then he found two extra pillows from the closet and put them under her ankle. Scooping some ice from the ice bucket on the table, he wrapped it in a towel from the bathroom and pressed it gently but firmly against her ankle.

"How's that?" he asked watching her anxiously from her bedside.

Anne nodded gratefully. Her ankle was cold, but the rest of her was gradually warming up. She couldn't believe he'd rescued her just as she'd dreamed he would. Just when she was about to give up. She didn't think she was going to die. She just thought she'd be there all night, half-buried in sand until someone stumbled across her the next day. That she was here, with Rafik, being cared for so expertly, seemed like a miracle.

"How did you know where I was?" she asked.

"I didn't. I just knew you weren't in your cabin or anywhere else I looked. One person said they'd seen someone on the beach. I thought it might be you. I had no other choice but to look there. Which reminds me that I should call your friends. I went to their cabin looking for you.''

''You could have gone to dinner or just…just forgotten about me.'' Her voice trembled as she said the last few words. If he had, she'd still be there, lost, alone, hurt, frightened… ''I can't believe you came out looking for me.''

''What did you think I'd do? There's no way I could forget about you.''

She managed a weak smile. She didn't know how to thank him so she didn't even try. When she felt better, she would. But now she had another question.

''How do you know how to do…'' She waved her hand in the direction of the pillows, the ice and her ankle, ''…this.''

''Just common sense,'' he said modestly. But he wasn't through yet. Another trip to the bathroom and he came back with a glass of water and two aspirins. ''For the pain and the swelling.''

She swallowed the pills and finished the glass of water.

''You must be hungry,'' he said. ''I'll order us some food and something hot to drink.''

''The kitchen might be closed by now.'' She had no idea what time it was, and it seemed almost too much of an effort to even look at her watch.

''Don't worry.''

Her eyes drifted shut for a few moments. She heard Rafik speaking quietly into his cell phone, but her tired brain made no sense of what he was saying. All she knew was that she had the sense that he had everything under control. She'd never felt so cared for, so safe as she did with him. Of course ordering dinner or finding a doctor who'd make house calls were easier when you had plenty of money. But money had nothing to do with him rescuing her on the beach. That took fortitude and strength and caring enough to make the effort.

She didn't know anyone else who would have come out in the dark looking for her on the off chance she might be out there. She told herself it wasn't just for her. She thought he was the kind of man who'd do it for anyone who needed rescuing. She was ashamed to think of how she'd wished he'd go home today. If he had, where would she be right now? She feared she'd still be out there on the sand.

She watched him behind heavy-lidded eyes as he pulled a chair next to the bed. Watched him shut the curtains, heard him running water in the bathroom. She doubted he'd find a doctor at any price, but he did. The physician was young and capable and looked nothing like any doctor she'd ever seen. Instead of a white coat he was in jeans and a jacket. He said he'd been on a friend's boat in the harbor when he'd been paged. He was new to the practice and got the worst call schedule—Saturday nights and Sundays. He seemed to be relieved to see she only suffered from a sprained ankle. He said Saturday-night emergencies were often gunshot wounds or motorcycle accidents.

"Your wife is going to have to stay off her ankle for a week or so," he told Rafik. Anne felt herself blushing furiously. Fortunately, no one was looking at her face. No one corrected him. She opened her mouth to tell them they weren't married, but it didn't seem to be worth the trouble. Both the doctor and Rafik were focused on her ankle.

"Tomorrow it will look even worse than it does today," the doctor continued. "But that's part of the healing process." He talked about getting a tensor bandage, about ice and elevation. He told her she could hobble to the bathroom but otherwise to stay right there in bed. She tried to tell him this was not her room, that she couldn't stay there in Rafik's bed, she'd already been there and done that—to disastrous results, but somehow the words just wouldn't come. Before he left, Rafik told the doctor to send him the bill. This time she was able to speak up and tell him she had health insurance, but he was already at the door and didn't appear to hear her.

After he'd gone, she told Rafik the doctor didn't understand the situation... "For some reason he thought we were married."

"I can't really blame him, can you?" Rafik asked. "Here we are in the same cabin."

"Yes, here we are."

"I notice you didn't correct him," Rafik said.

"Neither did you," she said. "In any case, I certainly intend to go back to my cabin."

"And disobey the doctor's orders?" he asked incredulously. "I'm afraid I can't permit that."

"I think he was being overly cautious," she said. "I can't spend the night here. I have to go back."

"You can't walk, that's for certain and I'm afraid I can't carry you there tonight. I think I might have strained my back out there on the beach."

"Oh, no. This is my fault. You should have told the doctor."

"I'll be fine in the morning," he assured her. "Now just relax. The food will be along any minute." He shoved the small table next to the bed and sure enough, the food arrived, carried by a uniformed delivery man. He brought in covered dishes and stacked them on the table. He brought plates and silverware and glasses.

While Anne watched dumbfounded, he uncovered the dishes, served soup in wide bowls, then wished them "Bon appetit!'' and left promising to return the next morning for the dishes.

"It smells wonderful," Anne said. Until that moment she hadn't realized how hungry she was. "Where did he come from? How did you arrange this?"

"Very simple. I just made a few calls. Many restaurants deliver, you know."

"No, I didn't know," she said. The idea of ordering food to be delivered from a restaurant was totally unknown to her. Not only must it be prohibitively expensive, under normal circumstances, there was no need. She told herself these were not normal circumstances. Dining with a sheik in his bed. Having him wrap her ankle, call a doctor, order food, prop the pillows on her lap and set her soup there, all that was most abnormal. And very luxurious. Almost worth spraining an ankle for. But not quite. Sipping a delicious broth made her almost forget about her ankle. Or the consequences.

"This is wonderful," she said. She would worry about her ankle later.

"Not bad," he agreed. He sat down next to the bed so he could eat next to her and serve her food. "How are you feeling?"

"Much better," she said. "I'd almost forgotten about my ankle. The pills must be kicking in. That and the hot food." And you, she wanted to say. She felt surrounded by the warmth of his presence, by his soothing voice and his calm capability. He gave her the sense that things would be all right. That all her problems could be solved. Rafik had a way of making her feel she was in good hands. She'd never felt so cared for. Was it only last night she'd been thinking how rich and spoiled he was? He might be rich, of course he *was* rich, but he was also the most thoughtful man she'd ever known.

Who else would have gone looking for her and when he found her hurt his own back by carrying her what seemed like miles across the beach? No one. And now he was doing everything for her as if she meant something to him. Maybe he felt he owed her a debt for pretending to be his fiancée. But he didn't. It had served them both equally. But now it was time for the charade to be over. She must tell him that. Not yet. Not while he was spooning some sauce onto her dinner plate around the lamb chops and rice pilaf and creamed spinach.

She ate slowly, savoring every bite.

"I'm proud of you," he said when she finally set her fork down. "You cleaned your plate, so you can have dessert."

"Dessert?" she asked, lying back against the pillow and closing her eyes. "All this and heaven, too."

"You're easy to please," he said.

She opened her eyes and met his gaze. "I've never had dinner in bed before."

"I understand there are many other things you've never done in bed before," he said. Then he caught himself. "I'm sorry. I shouldn't have brought it up again. You made your position quite clear last night."

"Rafik…"

"I understand," he said, "and I respect your morals. Now let's see what they've brought for dessert."

The dessert was a combination of many small things. A tiny chocolate mousse, an apple dumpling with caramel sauce, one perfect slice of tiramisu. She couldn't imagine what such a dinner must have cost him. She had a bite of each along with coffee. He smiled proudly at her as if she'd done something wonderful by eating so much, then he removed the dishes and put the table back next to the window. She knew she should insist on returning to her cabin, but she sensed he'd resist, and that he'd win. She wanted to ask him where he'd sleep, but she was afraid to hear him say he'd sleep in the chair.

Next he ran a hot bath for her, helped her hobble into the bathroom, supplied her with one of his clean shirts and left her alone in the bathroom. She could hear the muted sounds of the television set in the background as she propped her ankle on the rim of the tub and felt the hot water seep into her body.

Getting in and out of the tub without bumping her ankle was a difficult process and seemed to take ages. She knew then she couldn't go any farther than his bed tonight no matter how wrong it was. No matter how many people knew about it. Wrapping his well-pressed cotton shirt around her was almost like being enveloped in his arms with his masculine scent surrounding her.

Rafik turned when he heard the bathroom door open. Anne came out in a cloud of steam, her red-gold hair in a damp tangle. Wearing his shirt, which grazed her knees, she was delectable. He took a deep breath to try to rid himself of the lecherous thoughts that rushed at him like the tides out there on the beach.

He had arranged the blankets so she could lie under them and still have her foot elevated.

"What about you?" she asked, drawing the sheet up to her chin.

"Don't worry about me," he assured her. "I'm not tired. I'll be fine in the chair."

"The chair?" she said. "Not with your back. The muscles will tighten up and you'll get worse."

His back. He'd forgotten he'd made up that story. There was nothing wrong with his back, but he certainly didn't want to sit up all night. Still...

''There's plenty of room in the bed for both of us,'' she said.

He'd imagined her saying those very words, so when she actually did, he wasn't sure he'd heard her right until she patted the area next to her pillow. He had to admit the king-sized bed looked big enough for two people even if they weren't engaged, married or in love. Since neither of them fell into any of those categories there was nothing to worry about, was there? Of course he had to admit he lusted after Anne's body, and he thought she felt an attraction to him. But given her moral standards, he wasn't going to do anything about his lust problem except try to ignore it.

Being in bed with her might not be the best way to ignore it. But right now he was too tired to protest. So he shrugged casually, though he felt anything but casual, and went to take a shower. By the time he got out, she was asleep. The memories of that first night came flooding back. At the time he'd thought she looked beautiful with her hair spread out on the pillow. Now she was even lovelier. But then, he'd thought that before. Once at the gala ball, then in her garden. Come to think of it, each time he saw her he was convinced she was more beautiful than the last time.

Very carefully, so as not to wake her, he crawled into his side of the bed. Instead of looking at her, he deliberately faced the wall. He didn't dare even glance her way. It was bad enough to smell the soap she'd used, the sweet smell of her skin and her hair. Bad enough to imagine touching her soft skin, holding her in his arms all night. He forced his eyes closed, but the images continued. He saw her on the beach, a crumpled form and he shuddered to think what would have happened if he hadn't found her. But he had. She was safe and sound in his bed. What would it be like if she were there every night? If he could make love to her every night?

He shifted his body and told himself to stop dreaming. There was no way Anne would ever be in his bed again, and most certainly she would never make love with him unless he married her. Married her. That's what his parents thought was going to happen. They thought he'd actually found the woman of his dreams. Maybe he had. But there was no way he was getting married. Of course Anne was special. But so was his last fiancée. Or so he'd thought. His parents had been just as crazy about her as they were about Anne. Just as certain he'd made the right choice. Of course it wasn't his choice at all, it was theirs.

It was only by luck he'd discovered the true nature of his fiancée before they got married. Marriage was forever. If and when he ever got married, he intended to stay married. It was better not to take a chance and ruin his life. Tomorrow he and Anne would decide how best to end this engagement. He was sure she'd be more than happy to see it end. It hadn't been easy for her to live a lie any more than it had for him. With this decision made, he finally fell asleep.

When Anne awoke Rafik was already up and dressed. She thought he'd slept next to her in bed, but she couldn't tell. Not by any indentation in the pillow or by the expression on his face. He'd already been out to get some flaky croissants and coffee for them when she woke up. "You're going to spoil me," she said as he spread a towel across a pillow and put it in her lap so she could eat in bed.

"I'm trying," he said, "but I don't think it's possible."

"The doctor was right," Anne said after she'd finished her coffee and examined her ankle. "It looks even worse today." It was swollen and discolored. She sat there looking at it in dismay.

When her friend Jean came to see how she was, she threw a blanket over her leg.

"It's nothing," Anne said. "Just a sprain. But it looks awful."

"What a shame," Jean said, sitting on the edge of the bed. "You'll miss the brunch this morning and the closing remarks. I suppose you'll be heading back to town soon?"

Anne looked at Rafik and he nodded. He asked Anne for the key to her cabin and went to pick up her belongings.

"When Rafik called us last night to say he'd found you I was so relieved. And so was he. He was so worried about you. I'd say frantic, but that wasn't it. He was just determined to find you."

"I...I can't believe he did find me. I was lying there in the sand thinking I'd be spending the night there...feeling stupid for going off like that by myself."

"It's been quite a weekend for you," Jean said.

Anne couldn't have agreed more. If Jean only knew the half of it. This weekend, she'd almost been seduced. She'd turned down an offer from a man she was wildly attracted to. She'd faced hypothermia and an injury last night on the beach. She'd been rescued and now she had a new perspective on Rafik. He was not the arrogant, spoiled, rich man she once thought. Instead he was kind and caring. He was extremely confident, but he had a right to be. He was the kind of man a woman would be lucky to have for a fiancé. But he wasn't hers. He never would be, no matter how much his parents wanted it. No matter how much she wanted it.

Chapter Nine

On the ride home Anne was as comfortable as Rafik could make her. He'd moved the passenger seat back so she could recline and elevate her foot. They talked about everything and nothing as he drove along the two-lane scenic highway. No mention was made of their so-called engagement, though it was on Anne's mind, and she was sure it wasn't far from Rafik's either. Somehow, sometime, something was going to have to happen.

That something was the cancellation of their engagement. She couldn't bring herself to mention it. It was so nice just to sit there and watch the green fields on one side and the ocean on the other and not think about the problems on the horizon. She enjoyed Rafik's conversation. She'd never realized he knew so much about so many things. About the tides and the weather and the crops that grew in the farms alongside of the road.

She was almost disappointed when the ride ended, and he brought her home to her house. Never had three hours passed so quickly. He insisted on carrying her inside, though she told him she could easily hobble in by herself. She sat on the couch with her leg stretched out in front of her while he brought her suitcases in.

She thanked him profusely and told him she'd be fine. She promised to stay off her foot as much as possible. She assured him she had a freezer full of food and that her bedroom was on the first floor so there was no danger of her climbing stairs or being on her feet for any length of time.

There was an awkward silence when she'd finished answering all his questions, while he stood in the middle of her living room looking around. He didn't seem to know whether to go or stay. He didn't seem to know what to say either or what to do. Which wasn't like him at all. As long as she'd known him, he was completely at ease in any social situation.

"All right," he said at last. "Call me if you need anything." He put her phone on the end table next to the couch, then he stood there for a long moment looking down at her as if he'd forgotten something. At that moment she almost told him not to go, but of course she didn't. There was no reason he should stay, none at all. No reason for her to tell him she didn't want him to leave, that she needed him, wanted him, didn't want to live without him. She could only imagine the look of panic on his face if she did. She had a sprained ankle but that didn't mean she needed a full-time nurse. She could take care of herself. She knew it and he knew it, too.

After a moment, he left. He hadn't touched her after he'd put her on the couch. It seemed to her that he'd stayed as far away as he could, as if she had some communicable disease instead of a sprained ankle. He didn't kiss her good-bye either. Not that she'd expected him to. It was just…it was just that it was so lonely, so unexpectedly lonely there without him.

She missed his voice, she missed his touch, the way he carried her with his arms wrapped around her. She missed having him in the same room with her. Missed knowing he was there for her. All that was over, she told herself. She lay on the couch listening to the sound of his car pulling away. She looked around her living room and a tear trickled down her cheek.

The silence was unbearable. Since she'd lived alone for years and had never been bothered by silence before, or by loneliness, she had to wonder what was wrong with her. She cleared her throat, and the sound echoed through the empty rooms. The house was empty and so was she. It was the kind of emptiness that no food can fill. She knew because they'd stopped for lunch at a drive-in. She thought, this is what it must be like to lose one's best friend. The tears and the emptiness, the utter bleakness of the future. A future without Rafik. She repeated to herself what she'd told Rafik. She had a life. She'd never looked for a man. Never felt unfulfilled, never yearned for a man in her life. No, she never had. Not until now.

He'd said he didn't think it was possible to spoil her, but he had. She was spoiled. In two days she'd been spoiled and she feared it might be a permanent condition. He'd rescued her, he'd taken care of her, he'd kissed her and he'd fed her. Yes, he tried to seduce her, but when she'd told him how she felt, he'd respected her. Night fell and she buried her face in the cushion on the couch and fell asleep.

Rafik went to the office the next day, determined not to think about Anne quite as much as he had. She'd assured him she'd be fine, that she'd call if she needed anything, but it had been many hours since he'd dropped her off, and he hadn't heard from her. When he saw his brother he told him what had happened over the weekend, excluding the part about Anne being a virgin and saving herself for marriage.

"So you did it, you took my advice," Rahman said with a self-satisfied smile. "You spent the weekend romancing her."

"Yes, you could say that, and now what am I supposed to do?" Rafik asked.

"That's obvious. You've got to take care of her. She's hurt, she's wounded. She needs you," Rahman said. "It's a perfect opportunity to make yourself indispensable."

"You think so? I'm not so sure. She's got an independent streak. I'm afraid of stepping over the boundaries she's set up. You should have heard what she said to me. She's not looking for a man in her life. She's not unfulfilled and she doesn't need anyone, and that means me."

"That's perfect," Rahman enthused, refusing to accept defeat. "She sounds like you. You're made for each other. You can continue this affair without strings until you get tired of each other."

Rafik winced at the word *affair*. "You're forgetting about the parents and the pressure they're putting on me to set a wedding date," he said. "Mother even gave me a family ring to give to Anne."

Rahman whistled between his teeth.

"So you see it's not as easy as you think. In fact, I think I'm at a dead end. I'm going to have to bite the bullet and break off the engagement which never was an engagement, anyway. It will hurt Mother and Father, but they'll get over it." He pictured their faces the night of the gala ball, how they'd watched Anne and him from across the dance floor, how they'd beamed at him. He thought of his mother entrusting the ring to him, thinking he'd finally found the woman of his heart.

Maybe he had, but how did one know? He'd been fooled before. He was not going to take a chance again.

"They'll get over it," Rahman said. "But will you?"

"Me? I never wanted to get engaged and I certainly don't want to get married. You of all people should appreciate that."

"Never? You mean you'll *never* get married?" Rahman asked.

"Who can say never?" Rafik said. "I only know how I feel now." But even as he said the words he realized he didn't know how he felt about marriage. All he knew was that right now he felt terrible. After only one weekend together, he missed her. He wanted to take care of her. Whether she wanted to be taken care of was the question. All he knew was that he had to see her.

"Hold down the fort," he said to his surprised brother. "I've got matters to attend to."

"Go for it," his brother murmured as Rafik walked out of the office.

When Anne didn't answer her front door, Rafik went around to the side and let himself in through the gate. When he saw her in her garden he was worried she'd disobeyed the doctor's orders and had resumed gardening. Then he saw she was sitting on the bench surrounded by flats of plants in plastic containers with her leg propped up. She was wearing a pair of faded blue jeans and a sweatshirt. Her hair was pulled back and fastened with a band. But small tendrils had escaped and brushed against her temples. He couldn't tell by the look on her face if she was glad to see him or not.

"How's your ankle?" he asked. He knelt down next to

her so he could look at it up close. It seemed more swollen and very discolored.

"It looks worse than it feels," she said.

"You haven't been walking on it, have you?"

"Not any farther than to this spot right here. But look." She waved her hand at the plants stacked up around the garden. "These native plants were delivered while I was gone. I'd actually forgotten how many I'd ordered. I should be planting them right now, but…"

"No, absolutely not," he said.

"I know, I know. It's so frustrating. I need to get them in the ground." She sighed. "I have so much work to do here. The summer is half over, my bird-watchers' group is meeting here in two weeks. I've told them about my garden and they're coming to see what you can do to attract birds to a garden in the city without using flowers which I'm allergic to. I thought I'd have a lot done by then, but now…."

"I'm sure they'll understand," he said.

"The bird-watchers will but the plants won't," she said. "They need to get established."

"Can I help?" he asked.

She looked him up and down, taking in his tailored suit and immaculate shirt and matching tie. "I don't think so."

"I have other clothes," he said.

"I'm sure you have none suitable for getting down on your knees in the dirt."

"Don't be too sure," he said. But she was right. He had nothing like that. But he could get some.

"Moreover, you don't have the time. Shouldn't you be at work?"

"Rahman can handle the work. It's good for him to have some responsibility. I'll just go get the proper clothes."

She put her hand on his arm. "Rafik, I can't impose on you this way. The plants can wait."

"You just said they need to get established." But Rafik was thinking more about himself than the plants. Compared to his office, this place offered solace and peace. More importantly, it offered a chance to spend more time with Anne in her garden. Also the smell of the lavender and of the damp earth satisfied something inside him he didn't know existed. Something very basic. He was beginning to realize why Anne was attracted to the soil. Maybe he'd even come to understand why she liked getting her hands dirty.

"Of course you'll have to tell me what to do," he said. "I've never done any gardening."

Before she could protest again, he left the garden. In the car he called Rahman and told him what needed to be done at the office.

"Wait a minute," Rahman said. "I'm on my way to lunch."

"This was your idea," Rafik reminded him. "I'm counting on you to fill in for me."

"For how long?" he asked.

"As long as it takes," Rafik said.

Rahman agreed reluctantly and Rafik went to a neighborhood thrift shop. He had never been to one before. The customers gave him more than one curious look as he sifted through the racks of jeans and shirts. He didn't want Anne to think he'd gone out and bought gardening clothes. He wanted her to think he'd simply gone home to change clothes. And that he was a regular guy and not a spoiled rich man.

He changed clothes in the small dressing room and gave himself a critical look in the mirror. He was pleased with the way the faded jeans fit him and the gray sweatshirt. He was pleased with everything except for the shoes. He needed some kind of sandals if he was to get the full effect and feel the dirt between his toes as Anne did. His next stop was a shoe store where he bought the kind of sturdy sandals he thought would be appropriate. He couldn't help the fact that they were new and not used.

On his way back to Anne's he picked up sandwiches and salads from a take-out shop. He'd been thoughtless not asking what food she needed. He was gratified by the look on Anne's face when he returned. She didn't say anything, she just looked him up and down, taking in the change in his appearance. She must have been surprised by his transformation, because obviously she'd never stopped thinking of him as a spoiled, rich sheik. But the clothes were only half the battle. Now that he looked the part, he had to be able to act the part as well, show her he could do what, in his country, only servants did.

After lunch in the garden, he began the job of digging, planting and watering, according to Anne's instructions. She was uncomfortable giving orders, at least at first. He had to admit he was a little uncomfortable getting them, too. He made mistakes. He uprooted some miners' lettuce, which he'd never heard of, thinking it was a weed. He trampled on a fern. But they settled into a routine. She'd point to a new plant and decide where to put it. He'd dig a hole and plant it. Then he'd surround it with fertilizer and mulch and water it.

At the end of the afternoon he wiped his brow and sat down next to her on the bench. He was tired, but it was a good feeling. Almost as good as the feeling he had after a few sets of handball.

"My mother told me you want to get married in your garden," he said.

"Oh, well, I was just, you know, talking off the top of my head. I have no intention..." She turned her head so he couldn't see her face, but not before he noticed her cheeks had turned pink.

"Why not?" He looked around. "The trellis would serve as the altar."

"I suppose it could, but I'm not getting married. I only said that because she asked me. I had to come up with something. I certainly couldn't picture getting married in the cathedral like Carolyn." She cleared her throat. "I can't thank you enough, Rafik. You've been so much help," Anne said.

He got the distinct impression she was trying to dismiss him. But he wasn't ready to be dismissed. "It looks like there's a lot more to do," he said.

"It can wait," she said.

"Why should it?" he asked. "I can come back tomorrow. That is if you want me to."

"Well of course, but..."

"Now let's see what's in that freezer of yours for dinner. All that work has made me hungry."

Before she could protest, he swooped her up in his arms and carried her into the house. He paused in the doorway and looked into her eyes. "I just want you to know," he said, "that if I ever did get engaged with the intention of getting married..."

"You don't have to explain," she said, cutting him off as if she didn't want to hear the end of the sentence. "I know how you feel. The next step is to get ourselves unengaged."

"Let's not talk about that until after you get back on your feet," he said. "In the meantime..." He trailed off without finishing his sentence. He knew what he wanted to do in the meantime. She was so close, her lips were only inches away, tempting him, torturing him. She was so warm, so soft, she smelled so sweet, like the fresh air in the garden. There was something in her eyes he'd never seen before. He would have called it seduction if he didn't know better.

Whatever it was, he kissed her once. He could have sworn that lightning struck, despite the fact there wasn't a cloud in the sky. She tightened her arms around his neck and kissed him back. This time it was thunder roaring in his ears.

It could have been gratitude that made her kiss him, but it wasn't that kind of kiss that said thank you. It was the kind that said kiss me again. So he did. Again and again until he staggered to the couch and fell back with her in his lap. She tasted just as good as the last time he'd kissed her, the night before he'd rescued her, but different. Something had changed.

She raked her hands through his hair and he shuddered.

"For a virgin," he said hoarsely, "you're a very sexy woman."

She blushed furiously. But a tiny smile tilted one corner of her mouth. A knowing smile that said she was aware of herself as a woman, a sexy woman at that. He hoped he'd had something to do with the change in her. Because she had changed. Whether she knew it or not, she was not the same woman he'd taken home from the wedding.

When he finally, reluctantly disentangled himself from her and propped up her ankle, he went to the kitchen to heat something for dinner, another thing he had scarcely ever done before in his life. There had been no need. There was always a restaurant, a food service, a hotel or a servant. But tonight he wanted to prove once again that he was not what she thought he was. Not what he once was.

He was amply repaid for his efforts by the wide-eyed look of surprise on her face when he appeared in the living room with two plates of food. Surprise and delight. He wanted to surprise and delight her every night. So he did, every night that week. With different dishes he ordered and had delivered, or prepared from what she had in her freezer.

When he insisted on returning day after day, Anne only managed a weak protest. When Rafik decided to do something, it was difficult to stop him. She should be grateful he was helping her so much. She *was* grateful. But she was worried, too. Worried that when it was over, and it would be over before long, she was going to suffer. Suffer more than she'd ever suffered before.

Because she'd fallen in love with him. Fallen in love with a sheik. It was so absurd it was ridiculous. She, an elementary schoolteacher who'd never had a ball gown, or attended a gala or mixed in high society, who'd never even had a serious boyfriend, much less a fiancé, was in love with a handsome, wealthy sheik. A man who had no intention of getting married to her or anyone.

She hadn't fallen in love with him because he was rich and handsome, she'd fallen in love with him because he was kind and thoughtful, intelligent, humorous and good company. As if it made any difference. It was hopeless. She knew it. He knew it, too. Though he didn't know how she felt, unless he was a mind reader.

She didn't know how much longer she could keep it a secret. If he stayed around planting in her garden much longer, she was going to have to be more careful. No kisses, no touching, no lingering looks. The best thing was to break off the engagement as soon as possible. He'd said he didn't want to talk about it until she was back on her feet. She prayed her recovery wouldn't take that long. But from the looks of her ankle today, she was worried.

As he worked with her day after day that week, she grew increasingly anxious. The more she saw of him, the more they worked together on the garden project, the closer she felt to him. She knew it was going to be hard to let him go, but she knew it was inevitable. By the end of the week both the garden and her ankle looked much better.

They were sitting at her kitchen table eating a dinner he'd put together as if they were an ordinary couple. His shirt was covered with grass stains. He looked nothing like the groomsman she'd spotted staring at her in the church the day of Carolyn's wedding. He looked like an ordinary man. But he was far from ordinary. Though she was able to walk now, he insisted on making her dinner and waiting on her. But that wasn't why she was so terribly, impossibly, madly in love with him. It was who he was and it was who she was when she was with him. She was having so much trouble keeping her love from showing, it made her heart hurt, if that was possible.

"We need to talk," she said, knowing she had to face the music. Knowing it wasn't going to get any easier.

"I thought we were talking," he said, pouring her a cup of coffee.

"I mean about our engagement. About, you know, how to dissolve it."

"Is that what you want to do?" he asked carefully.

"It doesn't matter what I want to do. It's what has to be done. We've been living a lie. It's not important to the people at my school, but your parents have got to know the truth."

He studied her face for a long moment. "All right, I'll tell them."

"What will you tell them?"

"That it didn't work out. What do they call it? Irreconcilable differences. A mutual agreement to disagree. Of course they won't be happy about it."

"They'll be angry with you."

"Probably. But I can handle them. We can still see each other, can't we?" he asked.

"What for?" She had to make a clean break. No more Rafik. If she sounded brusque, so be it. If she continued to see him, it would break her heart.

He looked taken aback. "I'll miss you," he said. "I can't imagine not seeing you. I guess you don't feel the same."

"Of course I'll miss you," she said, "but I can't depend on you forever. You've spoiled me terribly and I have to get back on my feet, both literally and figuratively. You've missed a week's worth of work. Don't you think it's time to get back to your life?"

"My life before you came into it? I can't remember what it was like."

"All the more reason for you to do whatever it is you do. Now that I can walk, I have to get caught up. The summer's half over and I haven't accomplished half of what I'd planned."

She was proud of herself for sounding so matter-of-fact. Proud of herself for not giving in to the tears that were building behind her eyes. That threatened to overwhelm her. She was afraid if he didn't go soon she'd fall apart. She'd beg him to stay. She'd implore him to stay engaged to her. She'd collapse under the weight of her secret love.

He got to his feet and leaned against the counter. "I guess I wasn't ready for this," he said. "I didn't realize how much I was holding you back."

"I didn't mean that," she said. "You've been a wonderful help to me and I'll never forget it. I'll never forget you."

He stared at her. His face paled under his bronzed skin. "That sounds like goodbye," he said.

She swallowed hard. She tried to say something, but the words wouldn't come. She didn't move. She couldn't, not when she felt like she was made of stone. If he kissed her she'd lose her composure altogether. She willed him to leave. Now. Without another word. Leave her to suffer alone. Leave him with a positive picture of her, cured of a sprained ankle and cured of her attachment to him. Free of pain. Back to normal. But she didn't know what normal was anymore.

He got the message. "Well, goodbye then, Anne. I wish you the best."

She forced a smile. "Thank you." She got up and walked him to the door.

This time she barely got the door shut before the tears came, rolling down her cheeks, hot and heavy. She'd got what she wanted. She'd gotten rid of Rafik. Forever. Yes, it hurt. But better now than later. She'd get over it. It was all a fantasy, anyway. A dream that couldn't come true. Falling in love with a sheik was doomed for failure, disappointment and let-down.

It would have been easier if she'd been teaching. If there had been a class of eager little children waiting for her each morning so that she'd have to get up and pull herself together. But it was summer vacation. She hosted the bird-watchers' group, heard them exclaim about what she'd done to the garden, heard them make suggestions about further plantings, but after they left, she felt let-down.

According to their suggestions, she made a list and ordered more plants from the nursery, so many they covered every available space, stacked high in her shed and on every plot of dirt. She might have overdone it, but that way the garden wouldn't feel empty without Rafik. So she thought. And it would provide her with a reason to get up in the morning.

Still she had to force herself to go to the garden every

morning. Once there, she'd sit and sip tea and stare at the chaos she'd created, overwhelmed by the amount of work she had to do, feeling more alone than she ever had in her life. It was his fault. His fault for making himself a part of her life. Her fault for letting him do it.

She turned off her phone just in case he tried to call her. If she heard his voice she might crumble. She might blurt out a confession that would embarrass them both. When there was a knock on her gate one morning, she jumped out of her bench. Her heart pounded like a jackhammer. But it wasn't Rafik.

It was Rafik's brother, Rahman. She felt all the air leave her lungs. She was crushed, but she was relieved as well.

"I tried to call you but I got a busy signal," he said.

"Come in," she said, opening the gate. "How are you?"

"I'm fine but the family is falling apart. Ever since Rafik told the parents he wasn't going to marry you."

"Oh, no. I hope he put at least half the blame on me. You know it wasn't all his idea to call it off."

"It wasn't? He said it was. He said he wanted to be a playboy again. You can imagine how that went over."

"Do you believe him?" she asked.

Rahman shook his head. "He's changed. I can't believe how he's changed. He's working night and day. And he's in a foul temper. You'd think Father would be pleased about his new work ethic, but he's not. He's furious with Rafik. He wants a daughter-in-law. He wants you." Rahman pointed his finger at Anne.

"But as you know, Rafik doesn't want a wife. He may not be a playboy anymore, but he still doesn't want to get married. He doesn't want me. Maybe if I went to see your father and explained that I can't marry Rafik. Not because he's a playboy but...but... No, I'll say I can't marry him because I don't love him."

"Don't you?"

She bit her lip. She couldn't lie anymore. Not to Rafik's brother. Not to anyone. What did it matter? It was over. All over.

"You don't need to answer," Rahman said. "I can see the answer in your eyes. Just as I thought."

"It doesn't matter how I feel," Anne said. "What's important is that I share the blame for this breakup. I knew it was going to happen from the beginning. I was a willing participant. Now I have to accept my responsibility. I'll go see your father and tell him…tell him something."

"It's worth a try," Rahman said.

The next day Anne dressed carefully in her one good suit and went to call on the old sheik. She didn't make an appointment, and she hoped to avoid running into Rafik. She was lucky. She didn't see Rafik, and she was ushered into the corner office where Rafik's father was in charge.

Massoud Harun stood up and greeted her warmly, asking her to sit down and offering to send for some tea. Anne shivered inside her suit jacket knowing that as soon as she'd spoken her piece, he wouldn't be feeling nearly so cordial toward her. Then he sat down and flexed his gnarled fingers thoughtfully for a long moment.

"To what do I owe the honor of this visit?" he asked finally in his usual formal manner.

"I feel it's my duty to tell you what happened between your son and me," she said. "I'm afraid you've been misinformed. It was I who called off the engagement."

"Oh?" he said.

She took a deep breath. "You see I have never been in love with Rafik."

Instead of being shocked, Sheik Massoud just nodded as if she'd said it looked like rain. "I understand that," his

father said. "In my country love is not a prerequisite for
marriage. Most often, as in my case, marriage is arranged
by the family, based on mutual respect and understanding.
Very often, love follows marriage. But this is America.
You're an American. If it wasn't love, then tell me why
you agreed to this engagement in the first place."

Anne's mind raced. She could have said she never had
agreed to it, that she'd been pressured into it by the very
man who was sitting opposite her. But she wasn't there to
make things worse, she was there to heal a family quarrel.
She should have had a backup plan, but she never dreamed
not being in love wasn't a good excuse for calling off an
engagement.

"For money," she said impulsively. "I wanted his
money."

The old sheik regarded her solemnly. "Money, is it?
How much?"

"Enough to buy acres of marshland for a bird sanctuary.
It would cost millions."

"Money is not a problem. Is money all you really
want?" His gaze was shrewd and intense.

Anne nodded and turned away, unable to look into his
eyes. He saw too much. Murmuring some excuse, she stood
and left the room. Blinded by tears she rushed down the
hall, out of the office and down the elevator. The only good
thing about the meeting was that she hadn't run into Rafik.
But what else had she accomplished by lying to an old
man? Nothing. She hadn't even made sense. She'd told him
she didn't love Rafik and that she only wanted his money.

His father was probably scratching his head right now
trying to understand why she'd broken the engagement. It
wasn't as if Rafik had gone bankrupt. He was still rich. As
his father said, money was not a problem. So what was the
problem? The problem was that she'd fallen in love with a

man who had no intention of getting married, and she had no intention of having an affair with him, even though he was the most attractive, the kindest and the sexiest man she'd ever met. But those were words she could never say to the man's father.

If Rafik thought hard work would impress his father he was wrong. He'd been working night and day since the day Anne told him not only did she want to dissolve their engagement, she didn't even want to see him anymore. He'd walked around in shock for a few days, then he'd decided to put his energies to work and try to forget about her. But he didn't forget about her, her face appeared before him when he least expected it. In the middle of a meeting, in the middle of the night when he tossed and turned in his bed trying to figure out what he'd done wrong. Trying to think of how he could persuade her to see him again. And his father continued to glower at him.

Until one day he called him into his office.

"I owe you an apology," his father said. "Your ex-fiancée was here to see me. She said it was her idea to terminate your engagement. You led me to think otherwise."

Anne, here? Anne came to see his father but not him? It shouldn't hurt so much to hear that, but it did. Why didn't she just thrust a knife in his chest and be done with it?

"Does it matter?" Rafik asked wearily.

"I think it does," his father said. "The woman told me the reason was she didn't love you."

"That's true," Rafik said. "Our engagement was based on mutual need. Not love." If she loved him she wouldn't have been so eager to call it off. She wouldn't have shoved him out of her life. She wouldn't have let him go so abruptly. She would have called him by now, told him how much she'd missed him, as he'd missed her. Or come to see him to tell him she couldn't live without him. Told him how she couldn't sleep at night just as he couldn't. She would have an ache in the middle of her chest as he did, a hollow feeling inside his ribs. She would not be able to eat, would have trouble concentrating. She wouldn't see the point in going on without him. That's how people felt when they were in love. He knew because he...he...*he* was in love. Absurdly, impossibly, unequivocally in love with Anne Sheridan. The realization hit him with the force of a thunderbolt.

Massoud got out of his chair. "Are you all right?" he asked anxiously. "You're pale. Let me get you a glass of water."

"Thank you," Rafik said, staring at the wall, but seeing nothing. Gratefully, he took the glass from his father and downed it.

"If I may continue," his father said. "She told me she wasn't in love with you, but I don't believe she was telling the truth."

"I'm afraid she was, Father," he said grimly.

"As you know, I'm somewhat of a student of human nature. Her words said one thing, but her face and her eyes said quite another. I believe she has fallen in love with you although she did not wish to admit it to me. Instead she invented a story about being after your money so she could have a bird refuge."

"Very creative, but neither is true. She made it quite clear that she doesn't love me and though she does want a bird refuge, she wasn't after me for my money. I'm quite sure of that."

"What do you intend to do about it?" his father asked.

"Buy her the bird refuge," Rafik said. "Though it must be our secret. If I have a chance to convince her to fall in

love with me, it must be for myself and not out of gratitude.''

"Of course," his father said. "But how...?"

Rafik shook his head. "I don't know how...I just know
I must try. Because life without Anne is miserable. The last
time I broke an engagement, or rather my fiancée broke it,
I felt only relief. So much relief I decided never to try
again. I would play the field and that way avoid another
situation like that. But this is different. Very different. I've
never felt the way I feel about Anne. I feel that I'm not
worthy. So before I go any further in my pursuit of her, I
intend to make a success of this business. I have to prove
to you, and myself and Anne that I'm not the playboy I
once was."

His father was unable to conceal his broad smile. He
patted his son on the back. "That's my boy," he said.

After Anne's conversation with Massoud Harun she was
at a loss to know what to do next. She turned her phone
back on because she thought she'd hear from someone in
his family. She thought she'd hear from Rahman at least,
telling her her attempt had failed. That his father still
blamed Rafik for their breakup. She thought she might hear
from Rafik, but why would he call her? He'd walked out
of her house and out of her life. Instead she got a call from
Sally, her bird-watching friend who'd helped her get ready
for the gala.

"Did you hear the news?" Sally asked breathlessly. She
didn't wait for an answer, she was too excited. "We got
the bird sanctuary. All twenty-five acres of marshland."

"I don't believe it," Anne said, sinking into a chair at
her kitchen table. "How...? Who...?"

"An anonymous donor," Sally said. "Isn't it wonderful?
All that land for the birds for nesting and feeding. All the

bake sales and car washes we had, raising nickels and dimes. Then someone comes along and buys the whole thing.''

''I thought we'd asked every foundation, every philanthropist around for the money. How did this happen out of the blue?''

''I don't know. I heard from Liz who heard from Andy who heard...I don't know,'' she repeated. ''And I don't think we ever will know. Some bird lover, obviously, who wants to remain anonymous.''

After she hung up, Anne went outside and paced up and down in her garden.

Money is not a problem, she heard the old man say. *Is money all you really want?*

Could it be? No, of course not. Why would he buy the marshland when his son wasn't going to marry her? Maybe as a consolation prize? *Though you tried to convince me otherwise, it was plain to see that you've fallen in love with my son. It was written all over your face. I'm sorry that he has no intention of marrying you, but you can have your marshland. Please don't think all sheiks are alike. Have a nice day.* No, that was ridiculous. Even rich people didn't throw their money around like that.

Anne decided to put such useless speculation out of her mind. Instead she hired two high school boys to help her with her garden. She intended to have it finished by the time school started in two weeks and she did. Throwing herself into the work, she told herself it had all been a dream—everything that had happened so far that summer. The dream was over. This was reality. The boys arrived every morning at eight and worked like demons. She made lunch for them and they all worked all afternoon. She knew people said that the young generation, Generation Y, was lazy, but whoever said that didn't know these boys. She tipped them handsomely at the end of the summer, and they went back to school with their wallets bulging as well as their muscles.

The garden looked wonderful. They'd paved a flagstone walkway, planted native plants that attracted birds and more fruit trees. The trellis was covered with vines.

I have a garden that I'm working on that would be perfect for a wedding.

Why had she ever first voiced that thought to Rafik's mother? Now she couldn't get it out of her mind. Couldn't stop imagining the chairs set up, the punch bowl, the minister in his black robe....

Anne went back to school with much relief, some eagerness and a little apprehension. On the first day, when the teachers got together in the lounge before class, she was able to deflect questions about her engagement. When asked about a wedding date, she was vague. She never said she wasn't engaged anymore, but it was obvious she didn't have a ring. And most people were too polite to pry.

Her students were a joy and the best she'd ever had. Of course she said that every year, but this year it was true. It was so good to look forward to school each day and to have lessons to prepare and papers to correct every evening. It left her less time to think about Rafik. To wonder if her talk with his father had done any good. She feared not. The old man had seemed to see right into her mind and know exactly what she was up to. She'd tried. But maybe she could have tried harder. She thought about the bird refuge, too, and wondered if she'd ever know who'd donated it.

A few weeks after school started, open house was held at Pinehurst School. It was a chance for parents to see what their child's teacher and her classroom looked like. Anne bought a new dress for the occasion. A simple sheath in a raspberry color with a matching cashmere cardigan. She wore it with a three-strand pearl choker and just for a moment as she stood in front of the mirror in her bedroom, giving herself a last critical look, she wished she were dressing for someone other than parents.

She remembered the anticipation she'd felt, the churning in her stomach, the weakness in her knees the last time she wore a new dress. The black dress she'd worn to the gala was tucked away in the back of her closet. She'd probably never have an opportunity to wear it again. Still, she wasn't sorry she'd bought it. The look in Rafik's eyes when he came to pick her up had been worth every penny she'd paid for it.

The campus looked beautiful that evening, lit by the occasional gas lamp. Her room was bright and cheerful and the parents all told her how happy their children were to be in her class.

She had just said goodbye to the last parent when she looked up to see Rafik standing in the doorway. She reached for something, anything to hold on to and desperately gripped the back of a chair with one shaking hand.

"Hello, Anne," he said. "You said I could come to the open house, remember?"

Remember? She remembered everything. Remembered him in her classroom after they'd told the whole staff they were engaged. Remembered how confused she'd felt. Afraid to care about him. Sure that he didn't care about her.

"Yes, of course," she said briskly. "I'm sorry, it's just about over. I was just getting ready to lock up."

"I wanted to talk to you for a moment, if you have time."

"Here?" Her voice almost cracked. Her heart was pounding, her face must be the color of her dress. She'd thought she'd never see him again, now he was here, in her classroom.

He nodded.

She made her way to her desk and sat down behind it. He leaned against the wall with his arms crossed.

"You're looking very lovely," he said solemnly. "That color becomes you."

"Thank you," she said. "You are, too. I mean, you look fine." Actually he looked almost pale, if someone who had a year-round tan could look pale, and as if he'd lost a few pounds. Her mind was spinning. Rafik here, in her school. Why, why, why?

"I'll get right to the point," he said. "I came to tell you that though I always said I would never get married, I've changed my mind."

Her heart fell. Rafik was getting married. Her lips felt so stiff she could barely speak. "Really?" she said. "Congratulations. I'm sure you'll be very happy."

"Are you? Are you sure, Anne? I wish I could be sure. The woman I'm in love with hasn't agreed to marry me yet."

She licked her lips. This was torture. Pure torture. Why was he doing this to her?

"In fact," he continued. "She almost threw me out of her house the last time I saw her."

"That's terrible," she murmured.

"That's not all. She told me to get back to my life. That I'd held her back from accomplishing what she had to do."

"I don't know why...what you want me to do about it."

"Do? I want you to tell me what to do. You're a woman. What do women want?"

"Did you tell her," Anne said. "Did you tell her how you felt?"

"You mean that's all there is to it? I just tell her that

I'm in love with her? That I fell in love with her the first time I saw her in her pink bridesmaid dress, but I didn't know it at the time? It took me days, weeks before I knew what had happened. It might have been the day she threw my money all over the floor, or the day I saw her in her garden with dirt on her toes, or the night I danced with her...."

Anne's eyes were full of tears. She couldn't move. She couldn't speak. She was overcome. She heard his words, but she couldn't believe them. She put her head down on her desk and sobbed.

He was across the room in a half a second. He sat on her desk and lifted her head so he could look into her face.

"Anne, stop. Stop crying. I'm sorry. I shouldn't have said it like that. I didn't know what to say, how to say it. I didn't mean to upset you. I just wanted to tell you how much I love you, to ask you, to beg you to marry me. If you don't, I don't know what I'll do. I'm not the same man you met at the wedding. I've changed. If you don't love me now, I understand. My father says love comes after marriage so there's always hope. Give me a chance. I beg you not to say no."

He stared at her, waiting, waiting for her answer. She blinked away her tears and managed a watery smile.

"Of course I'll marry you," she said softly. "I love you, too. I'm sorry I almost threw you out of my house, but I couldn't go on seeing you and knowing that you'd never marry me. It was too painful. You recall you were very determined...."

"Don't remind me," he groaned. "I was a fool. I had no idea what I was talking about. I'd never been in love. Never thought it would happen to me. Not until you came along. Not until we spent so much time together. Then suddenly you were gone out of my life. It was terrible. It was as if the sun stopped shining. I haven't been very good company, as my family will attest.''

"Tell me one thing, did *you* buy that marshland?'' she asked.

"Would you love me more if I did?'' he asked.

She shook her head. "I couldn't love you more,'' she said shyly. It would take a while before she could say things like that without blushing.

"I bought it, but I didn't want to buy your love,'' he explained. "I just wanted you to have it.'' He got off the desk and pulled her up into his arms.

She wound her arms around his neck and kissed him. He kissed her back, deeply, possessively. She grabbed fistfuls of his shirt and got lost in the rapture of his kiss. He loved her. It would take a while to get used to it. But she had time. She had a whole lifetime.

Epilogue

It was a small affair. Only the immediate families and a group of close friends attended the garden wedding of Sheik Rafik Harun and Anne Sheridan. The bride wore the groom's mother's wedding dress and walked slowly up a flagstone path to the strains of a string quartet playing the "Wedding March." The groom, who wore the traditional headdress as befitting his status, stood at the trellis which served as an altar. His eyes gleamed as his beautiful red-haired bride appeared from behind the foliage. His brother, who served as his best man, handed him the ring, which had been in the family for generations, to place on his bride's finger.

There were many tears that day. Tears of joy, tears of happiness and sentimental tears. But mostly there were smiles, toasts and congratulations as the caterers brought out trays of smoked salmon, crab cakes and brochettes of lamb. Everyone wanted to take credit for bringing the two together. Carolyn said it all started at her wedding. Rafik's father told his mother he knew about it before anyone else.

Jean declared Rafik to be the luckiest man alive. Rahman insisted that Rafik was luckier.

Only the newlyweds knew for sure who was the luckiest. As they winged their way to their honeymoon in Paris, they decided they were the luckiest couple in the world. And the happiest.

*   *   *   *   *

In her new miniseries,

DESTINY, TEXAS

Teresa Southwick

reveals what happens when a group of friends
return to their hometown: a place of lost loves,
budding dreams and enternal hope.

CRAZY FOR LOVIN' YOU
(SR #1529, July 2001)

THIS KISS
(SR #1541, September 2001)

IF YOU DON'T KNOW BY NOW
(SR #1560, December 2001)

and the final story
(SR #1572, February 2002)

Available at your favorite retail outlet.

Where love comes alive™

Visit Silhouette at www.eHarlequin.com   SRDES

CALL THE ONES YOU LOVE OVER THE HOLIDAYS!

Save $25 off future book purchases when you buy any four Harlequin® or Silhouette® books in October, November and December 2001,

PLUS

receive a phone card good for 15 minutes of long-distance calls to anyone you want in North America!

WHAT AN INCREDIBLE DEAL!

Just fill out this form and attach 4 proofs of purchase (cash register receipts) from October, November and December 2001 books, and Harlequin Books will send you a coupon booklet worth a total savings of $25 off future purchases of Harlequin® and Silhouette® books, AND a 15-minute phone card to call the ones you love, anywhere in North America.

Please send this form, along with your cash register receipts as proofs of purchase, to:
In the USA: Harlequin Books, P.O. Box 9057, Buffalo, NY 14269-9057
In Canada: Harlequin Books, P.O. Box 622, Fort Erie, Ontario L2A 5X3
Cash register receipts must be dated no later than December 31, 2001.
Limit of 1 coupon booklet and phone card per household.
Please allow 4-6 weeks for delivery.

I accept your offer! Please send me my coupon booklet and a 15-minute phone card:

Name: _____

Address: _____ City: _____

State/Prov.: _____ Zip/Postal Code: _____

Account Number (if available): _____

---

097 KJB DAGL
PHQ4012

If you enjoyed what you just read,
then we've got an offer you can't resist!

Take 2 bestselling love stories FREE!

Plus get a FREE surprise gift!

Celebrate the season with

Midnight Clear

A holiday anthology featuring
a classic Christmas story from
New York Times bestselling author

Debbie Macomber

Plus a brand-new *Morgan's Mercenaries* story
from *USA Today* bestselling author

Lindsay McKenna

And a brand-new *Twins on the Doorstep* story
from national bestselling author

Stella Bagwell

Available at your favorite retail outlets in November 2001!

Silhouette®
Where love comes alive™

Visit Silhouette at www.eHarlequin.com